SPUNKY BUMPKIN

SAM CHEEVER

ELECTRIC PROSE PUBLICATIONS

PRAISE FOR SAM CHEEVER

In a small country town, justice might be swift...but rumor is swifter!

My name is Joey and I'm just a simple country girl. Nothing special at all. Well, except for the fact that I tend to find bodies all over the place. But aside from that I'm just like everybody else.

Oh, then there's that really big secret in my past. The one that involves my parents dying in a fiery crash and me finding out that the person who caused their deaths might be after me too.

But none of that matters right now. What matters

is that I have a problem. My friend, Deputy Arno Willager just arrested his mom for murder.

He's devastated. And to make his problems worse, his mom's beloved elderly dog is in bad shape. Yeah, long story, we'll get into that later.

Arno's mom...well...unfortunately she can't remember a thing. So Hal and I—oh, Hal's my boyfriend and he's a PI—are trying to help Arno figure out who killed the troublemaker his mom was standing over with a bloody knife. Yeah, it's quite a mess.

But with the help of my best friend Caphy (my Pitbull) and Hal, I'm pretty sure we can suss out a killer.

After all, we've done it a few times already!

I was a soggy, sobbing mess. I'd known I shouldn't let Hal talk me into watching a movie about a boy and his dog. That never ended well for the dog.

Hollyweird just loved making pet lovers miserable.

On the screen, the eighteen-year-old gave his sad-eyed dog, which had been at his side since he was a small boy, a negligent wave and walked out the door, heading off to college and new excitement... without his faithful canine companion.

The dog sank dejectedly to the boy's bed, nose on paws and liquid brown eyes sad enough to make a serial killer sob, and I broke down into loud, inconsolable sobbing of my own.

Hal looked alarmed. He tried to move closer to wrap an arm around my shoulders, but Caphy was having none of it. If there was consoling to do, she'd be the dog to do it.

After all, it had been the human male who'd gotten me into the mess, it would take a pibl to ease me out of it.

She'd jumped up onto the couch between us at the start of the movie, draping her heavy form across my lap as if she'd known we needed to store up a good dose of canine comfort, and she wasn't letting anybody near me as I completely fell apart.

She'd even given LaLee a low growl, the hair on her back rising to reinforce the warning.

I wrapped my arms around her and buried my face in her sweet-smelling fur, sobbing uncontrollably.

Hal's big, warm hand found my shoulder and patted ineffectually. He clicked off the movie, and the room fell silent except for my sniffling and the occasional hiccupping sob.

I could feel Hal's regret like a vibration on the air.

I finally stopped crying and lifted my head, running the heel of my hand across my cheeks to sop up some of the copious moisture there.

Hal wordlessly handed me his pristine handkerchief.

"Thank you," I said in a tear-clogged voice. "Sorry."

He shook his head, squeezing my shoulder,

which was the only part of my body Caphy was allowing him to touch. "It's my fault. You tried to warn me."

I gave a watery laugh. "I did."

A deep rumble sounded behind me, and I turned my head to see LaLee had moved closer. She sat like a Sphinx on the back of the couch, her pretty blue gaze locked onto mine. "Hey, girl." The cat reached out a paw and touched my cheek, not even releasing her claws as she did.

It was a huge concession for her and I deeply appreciated it.

I smiled, sniffling loudly. "Thanks, LaLee."

Hal got up to get me some water, and I lay my head back, feeling drained from my cry-athon as well as from the deep sadness spurred inside me by the movie. I'd never understand why people liked to watch sad movies. All they did was drain me of energy and leave me feeling depressed.

My phone rang, making me jump. I glanced at the old-fashioned wall clock above the TV. Eleven o'clock at night. Who in the world would be calling me?

Then I realized it might be my mom and jumped on my cell phone without looking at the ID.

"Hello?"

"Joey." His voice was raw, broken, and I sat immediately upright. "Arno? What's wrong?"

Hal came in carrying my glass of water and

looked a question at me. I shook my head to let him know I had no idea.

Silence was the only response Arno gave me.

My mind formed a picture of the Deputy lying broken in a ditch somewhere. I gently shoved Caphy off my lap and stood. "Arno, talk to me. Are you okay?"

"She..." Arno took a deep, trembling breath, clearly struggling to say what needed to be said.

I slipped into the flip-flops I'd kicked nearly under the couch. "Tell me where you are. Hal and I will come to you."

Another short silence broke on the sound of Arno clearing his throat. "Twenty-five Sixteen Antler's Way. Hurry."

"We'll be there in five minutes. Arno?"

I waited for him to respond. "Yeah?"

"Whatever it is, it's going to be all right. Okay?"

He took a shuddering breath. "I'm not so sure about that, Joey."

My heart pounded against my ribs. I'd never heard my friend sound so broken. I looked at Hal and he must have seen the worry in my eyes. He nodded, pulling his keys from his pocket. "Come on. I'll drive."

Caphy jumped down from the couch and trotted along behind us as we headed for the front door.

Hal's dark blue SUV waited in the drive at the base of the steps, a dark bulk in the yellow illumination of my porch light. I let Caphy into the back seat and climbed in front as the big car started up with a throaty rumble.

Hal put it into gear and shot around the circle and into the driveway, big tires sending gravel up in a spray as he pulled out onto Goat's Hollow Road. "Where am I going?"

"Head into Deer Hollow. He's on Antler's Way." I thought about the short road that jutted off Main Street at the edge of town. It was a residential street, a strange mix of nice homes, broken-down clapboard houses, and a couple of double-wide trailers.

There was something else about the street that niggled, but for the life of me, I couldn't think what it was. "He sounded terrible, Hal."

My handsome PI reached across the space between us and clasped my icy hand in his big warm grip. "Arno's a strong, capable guy, Joey. Whatever's going on, he'll be fine."

I nodded, clinging to his assurances even though I knew he was just trying to make me feel better. I'd learned when my parents' plane had gone down that kind words and gentle reassurances could sometimes be a bulwark against total devastation.

As if she could read my mind, Caphy whined softly, settling her heavy head onto my shoulder.

I smiled. "Thanks, girl." I turned my head and kissed the soft warmth of her wide muzzle.

"Did Arno tell you what's going on?" Hal asked

as we shot past the sign announcing the Deer Hollow city limits.

"No. He was struggling to say anything." I frowned. That was the thing that scared me the most. He'd sounded so completely devastated. I couldn't imagine what would take Arno Willager to his knees like that. Hal was right. Arno was strong and capable. I'd rarely seen even the smallest crack in his armor. There were only a few things that had the potential to devastate the deputy that way. Maybe only one.

And at that moment, I had a flash of intuition. I knew why the address sounded so familiar.

Arno's mother lived there.

Hal slowed and turned the SUV onto Antler's Way. The entire street was only two city blocks long and ended in a cul-de-sac. Straight ahead, in the center of the cul-de-sac, was a worn-down double-wide trailer with a separate two-car garage. Lights flashed into the night from three Sheriff's vehicles that looked like they'd pulled up and skidded to an abrupt stop. I half expected to see deputies squatting behind car doors with guns drawn.

Hal and I jumped from the SUV, leaving Caphy in the car until I knew what was going on.

She whined unhappily, her big paws slamming against the glass of the side window as we jogged toward the spot where Arno stood, head lowered and hands on his hips.

He was alone in a quiet spot in the night. An island of false calm in a sea of roiling activity. I knew as soon as he lifted his head, his eyes boring into mine, that he was about as far from calm as he could get.

"What's going on?" I asked gently.

His gaze slid to the pickup truck I hadn't noticed off to the side. I followed his line of sight and frowned when I saw her. Mrs. Willager stared out at us, her gaze filled with the calm her son couldn't seem to find.

"Your mother? Is she okay? Do you need us to take her to the hospital?"

Arno shook his head, a single, violent jerk. "I need you to take Spunky to the vet."

I blinked a few times, completely taken aback by his strange request. "Excuse me?"

Arno scrubbed a hand over his chin, the bristly sound breaking through the silence of the night. "She's..." He frowned. "I think someone's poisoned her." He jerked his head toward the grass beneath a large tree.

Arno's coat covered something in that spot, a fringe of golden tail sticking out from underneath it. I hurried over and dropped to my knees beside the dog. Spunky's eyes were open, and her muzzle was painted in yellow foam. She whined softly as I ran my hand over her wide head. "What's wrong, girl?"

A large form moved up behind me, and I looked up at Hal, tears burning my eyes. "She's really sick."

He nodded, touching my shoulder. "Let me grab her, Joey. We need to get her to Doc Beetle."

Arno showed up behind Hal as I straightened, sniffling. "I already called him. He's expecting you," he said.

Hal scooped up the big golden retriever as if she weighed nothing and headed for his car.

I looked toward the broken-down garage, where Arno's gaze seemed stuck, his face devoid of its usual healthy color. Someone was lying on the broken concrete in front of the rickety structure. The deputies had covered the body with what looked like a painting tarp, but two large boots stuck out from one end.

I looked back at Arno. "Is he the one who poisoned her?"

Arno closed his eyes for a beat, then nodded. "Probably." He opened his eyes again and fixed them on me. "It looks like she killed him, Joey."

"She?" I asked as horror bloomed in my chest. "Spunky?"

He gave a short bark of laughter that had no humor in it. "No. My mom. It looks to me like he poisoned her dog, and she stabbed him with a kitchen knife."

2

There was a really good chance that Doc Beetle was over a hundred years old. I remembered him being old and bent when I was a little girl, and that was a couple of decades ago. Doc ran bony, gnarled hands over the big retriever's heaving sides and spoke soft words of encouragement as he took her temperature.

It was a measure of her misery that she didn't even perk an ear when he slid the thermometer into her rear regions. Caphy always jumped a little and cast an accusing glare over her shoulder when he did it to her.

Pressed against my leg with a worried expression on her face, my pibl whined softly in commiseration for her new friend.

"Is she going to be all right?" I asked the cranky old vet.

He slid a glare of his own up to my face, his brown eyes looking like accusatory pebbles in his small, wizened face.

I chewed the inside of my lip, fearful of the sweet dog's condition, but even more fearful of annoying the veterinarian.

He read the thermometer and frowned, sighing softly. "She'll need to stay here." He filled two needles from the bottles he kept in a cabinet above the sink and injected her with the contents.

Spunky didn't even twitch. She lay there panting and listless, her tongue an unhealthy light pink. Moving more quickly than seemed possible given his near-fossilized state, the doc shaved a spot on the retriever's front leg and squirted alcohol onto the area. He inserted an IV, taping it around her leg and then coiling the remaining line as he glanced at Hal. "Can I trouble you to carry the old girl for me?"

"Of course, Doc." Hal gently scooped her up, making it look easy even as his biceps bulged from her weight.

"This way," Doc Beetle instructed.

We followed him through a door I'd never gone through and into a room with a narrow bed for a human and a large bed with bumpers for the patient. Doc Beetle pointed to the dog bed. "Lay her down there. I'll hook this up and we'll get fluids running through her."

I stood in the doorway, twining my fingers and feeling helpless. "Doc Beetle..." I finally asked.

He skimmed me another look, only slightly less hostile. "I don't know, Joey," he said to my unasked question. "Our goal right now is to get her through the night." He glanced at a big, round clock on the wall, the numbers oversized as if to accommodate his older-than-dirt eyesight. "What's left of it..."

I glanced at the clock too, amazed to see that it was already after midnight. "You'll call?"

"I'll call the dog's owner." He hooked an IV bag over the pole situated next to the bed, frowning.

Hal and I shared a long look. "That might be a problem," Hal finally said.

Doc's caterpillar-like eyebrows lowered over his small eyes. He looked at me. "Is Mary all right?"

I caught the inside of my lower lip between my teeth, unsure how much Arno would want me to reveal. Finally, I said, "She's at the police station. Her neighbor was killed tonight, and they're interviewing her about it."

I hoped he'd assume I meant as a witness rather than a suspect. After a long pause, he asked, "Which neighbor?"

I shrugged. "I don't know his name, sorry."

"He lives at the top of the cul-de-sac," Hal told the veterinarian. "In a double-wide with a detached garage."

"Viper Branch," Doc said, the lines on his brow

deepening. "Nasty piece of work, that guy." Doc's gaze turned shrewd. "He the one who poisoned this sweet, old girl?"

Leave it to Doc to put the pieces of the puzzle together and come up with the unspoken truth.

"That's the current theory," Hal said evasively. "Do you think he's capable?"

Doc ran a hand over the dark-gray bristles on his cheeks. A soft rasping sound accompanied the action. "More than capable. He's done it before."

I felt my eyes go wide. "He's poisoned Spunky?"

"Not Spunky," Doc said, his gaze falling to the sleeping dog and softening. "And not poison. When he was a kid, only sixteen or so, his family lived on a plot of land out off Highway 37. The neighbor's cattle kept escaping the fence and wandering onto the Branch property. The boy shot one of them with his dad's hunting rifle." Doc shook his head. "Sheriff at the time, Decker I think his name was, gave Viper thirty days community service and made him pay the neighbor back for the cow." Doc bent with an alarming creaking sound and grasped Spunky's leg between two fingers, observing his watch as he presumably took her heart rate.

Hal and I stayed quiet until he straightened again with a groan. He continued his story as if he'd never paused. "Everybody thought he'd learned his lesson. Until raccoons and possum started showing up dead around the Branch place." Doc sighed. He glanced toward me, his expression weary. "I'm guessing Mary killed him?"

My shock must have shown on my face. He gave me a rusty-looking smile. "I know everybody in this town, young lady. All their secrets. All their little personality quirks. And I know that Mary Willager is tougher than her son gives her credit for. She loves this dog almost as much as she loves her own child." His weary gaze found the dog again. "She wouldn't just stand by and let someone get away with harming her."

"Arno's pretty upset," I offered, not verifying Doc's assessment of the situation but not denying it either.

He nodded. "I can imagine. All right, I'll call you in the morning and give you a report. You'll pass it on to Mary?"

Or someone with the last name Willager, I thought as I nodded. "Thanks, Doc."

Caphy came into the room and walked over to Spunky, sniffing her head and then bathing one of her floppy ears, her tail wagging.

Watching her, Doc Beetle smiled one of his rare smiles. "She'll be all right, Caphy girl."

Caphy looked up at him, whippet-like tail twitching with uncertainty. Her pretty green eyes were filled with worry. Doc reached down and framed her face with his gnarled hands, bending to put his face close to hers. "I'll take good care of your friend. I promise."

Caphy swiped a wide, pink tongue over his nose and her tail gave a relieved wag, thumping hard against the wall.

I relaxed slightly. Caphy believed Doc would pull Spunky through and she was an excellent judge of character. So, I decided I'd believe it too.

If nothing else, it would make getting through the next task a little bit easier. I waited until we were back in the car and Hal was heading out of the parking lot before opening my mouth to tell him I wanted to talk to Mary Willager.

I never got the chance.

Hal turned to me before exiting the lot. "Shall we go see Mary then?"

My mouth slammed closed and a warm feeling swept through me. It was nice being with someone who understood me so well.

I nodded, giving him a grateful smile. Hal turned the big car toward the highway and the County Sheriff's building just outside of town.

rno was standing in the hallway adjacent to the bullpen, staring at a door to one of the interview rooms. He was lost in

thought, not even looking up as Hal and I came up behind him.

I lifted my hand to touch his shoulder, warning him we were there, but my hand stopped several inches away. His pain was so visceral it was like a living barrier pulsing around his tall form.

He sighed, lowering his head. "I've been trying to work up the courage to go in there."

Hal and I shared a look. He'd known we were there without even looking at us.

I let my hand fall to his shoulder, giving it a commiserating squeeze. "I'm so sorry, Arno."

His gaze whipped around, finding me. "We have to prove she didn't kill him, Joey." His voice was a razor, cutting the tension surrounding him like a knife. But it was his gaze that had me taking a step back.

It was filled with such rage.

He saw me flinch and closed his eyes, pulling air into his lungs as Hal took a small step closer, ready to intervene if he needed to.

"You can't be part of this investigation, Willager," Hal said softly. "You know that, right?"

Fists clenched and eyes still closed, Arno's broad shoulders stiffened, and I thought he was going to start swinging.

"Arno," I said in warning.

He shook his head, opening his eyes. "I'm sorry. I know you're right, Amity. I just..." He slid another glance toward the door. "I couldn't put her in a cell. I just couldn't do it." Arno expelled air in a frustrated rush and turned his back to the door, finally meeting Hal's gaze. "You were a cop once. I trust you. I'd like you to talk to her, Amity. Take her statement."

Hal's eyes went wide. He was clearly shocked by Arno's request. "I don't think..."

"Please?" The word was wrenched from between Arno's stiff lips, filled with more pain than plea.

Hal accurately read the desperation giving the request its sour edge, and he was too kind of a person not to want to help. He inclined his head. "I'll interview her. But I'd like Joey there too."

I was certain Arno would reject my participation. But to my surprise, he nodded. "She likes Joey. It will help to have her there."

"Good," Hal said, sliding his gaze to me. "That okay with you?"

"Of course." I caught Arno's gaze. "We'll figure this out, Arno." Doc Beetle's words flitted through my brain as I tried to give Arno comfort.

I'm guessing Mary killed him?

Doc hadn't been lying when he'd said he knew everybody. He'd lived in Deer Hollow a long time. And if he believed Mary was capable of killing Viper Branch—well—his assessment would be more objective...less tainted by years of trying to protect a woman who probably never needed protecting.

3

---

*M*ary Willager was a tall woman, honed and lean from years of an active lifestyle and careful habits. Like her son, she was a serious person, viewing the world through a prism of self-formed rules that didn't offer a lot of flexibility.

She sat in a hard chair at the long table, her gaze focused on the hands entwined before her.

I noted that Arno hadn't slapped the cuffs on his mother. Not that I'd expected he would. The poor man couldn't even bring himself to put her in a cell.

Mary looked up as Hal and I came into the small, dark room.

Her complexion was pale, her lips compressed. She wore little makeup, her blonde brows nearly invisible against her pale skin. The cloud of short blonde hair was tidy, looking as if she'd just styled it, and she wore charcoal gray slacks and a black and white silk blouse that seemed a bit overdone for middle of the night murdering.

Dark spots speckled her clothing. I could only assume it was blood.

I gave the older woman a smile. "Hey, Mrs. Willager."

Mary's lips compressed and her brown eyes, so like her son's, turned shiny with unshed tears. "Hey, Joey."

Hal stepped past me and stopped next to the woman's chair, bending down and offering her his hand. "Mrs. Willager, I'm Hal Amity. Your son asked me to get your statement."

Nodding her understanding, she gave his hand a firm shake and released it. A single tear slipped down her cheek. "That's very kind. I'm afraid Arno's not taking this very well." She glanced at me and then back to Hal, her lips curving slightly upward. "You're Joey's new beau."

It wasn't a question, and Hal didn't treat it as one. "Can we get you anything before we start? A glass of water? Some tea?"

She shook her head. "No, thank you, dear. I'm fine."

Seeing the rigid way the older woman held herself, I thought "fine" was an overstatement. I slipped into a chair beside Mary and the other woman reached out to clasp my hand, squeezing it with a firmness that belied her outer calm.

Hal sat down across from us, arranging a lined pad in front of him. He pulled a pen from his shirt pocket and clicked it open. Then he placed the small recorder Arno had given him between us on the table. Before he started the recorder, he looked directly into Mary's eyes. "We are going to record this conversation, Mrs. Willager. Are you comfortable with that?"

Arno had told us that the Interview rooms were video-recorded as standard practice during an interview, but he'd wanted his mother to be aware she was being recorded, so he'd asked Hal to use the recorder.

I could tell by Hal's reaction that Arno's request bordered on tampering, but Hal agreed, though I thought a bit reluctantly, to use the device.

"Of course. Believe it or not, Mr. Amity, I want to get to the bottom of this as much as you do."

I blinked in surprise. Was Mary saying she hadn't killed Mr. Branch?

"But before we start," Mary's grip on my hand became painful. She looked across the table at Hal. "Have you heard about my baby girl?"

It took Hal a moment, but his expression finally cleared as he realized she was asking about her dog. He glanced toward me, and I got the message his dark gaze was sending.

Turning to Mary, I said, "Spunky's with Doc Beetle. He's given her something to make her comfortable and hooked her up to an IV. He said the goal is to get her through the next several hours." I left it there on purpose. There was no point in worrying Mary unnecessarily. If Spunky passed, we'd deal with it at that point.

To my great relief, Mary didn't press for details. She nodded. "Thank you, dear. I assume Arnold asked you to take her to Doc?"

I smiled. "I was happy we could help."

Mary stared at our clasped hands for a moment and then lifted a tear-drenched gaze to me. "If I..." she sniffed, dragging the back of her hand under her eyes. "If I'm not out of here by the time she gets released, could you keep her for me? I trust you and, I know your beautiful dog will be kind to her while she gets better."

I nodded without hesitation. "Of course. She can stay with me as long as she needs to. I'll enjoy having her. And Caphy's already gotten attached."

She smiled but there was little happiness in it. "Good." She turned to Hal, nodding toward the recorder.

He hit "Record" and sat with pen poised over paper as he began speaking for the benefit of the recording, introducing himself and his purpose there and giving Mary's full name.

Then he fixed an intense green gaze on Mary. His

voice was soft and kind as he asked the first question. "Mrs. Willager, what can you tell me about Viper Branch's death?"

Mary shrugged. "Not much. I have no idea how he died."

I barely kept from glancing toward Hal.

He went on without missing a beat. "How did you come to be at the scene?"

Mary frowned, her light-blonde brows knitting together. "I...to be honest I don't remember."

I skimmed a look to Hal, unable to resist gauging his response. He was busy jotting her response down onto the pad and didn't acknowledge my glance.

When he'd finished scribbling what looked like some kind of strange shorthand onto the page, he nodded, fixing her with another look. "You were found holding a knife, Mrs. Willager. It was covered in Mr. Branch's blood. Do you remember picking up the knife?"

She shuddered once and her slender throat worked over a hard swallow. But she jerked her head in a negative response.

"Can you vocalize your responses, please?" Hal reminded her.

"Yes. I mean, no, I don't remember picking up the knife, Mr. Amity. That's the thing..." She tugged her hand free of my grasp and held both hands in front of her, staring at her palms. For the first time, I saw the dark red stain of blood beneath her long nails.

Finally, she looked up at Hal as if suddenly remembering she hadn't finished her thought. "I don't remember anything at all from tonight. Nothing, beyond getting into my car at church and starting home." She shook her head, tears finally falling freely. "I don't even remember finding my poor sick girl in the yard." She broke down then, the idea that she'd somehow failed her dog the one thing from the night that she couldn't endure among all the others.

Even the possibility that she'd murdered a man.

In that moment I knew Doc Beetle had been right. Mary wouldn't take it well if Viper Branch had poisoned Spunky. In fact, all signs pointed to the possibility that she hadn't taken it well at all. She'd become so upset she'd apparently given herself stress-induced amnesia.

"You don't recall finding your dog and realizing she'd been poisoned?"

Mary shook her head, then seemed to remember she was being recorded and said, "No."

"You don't remember taking a knife from your kitchen?" Hal asked.

"No."

"You don't remember walking over to Viper Branch's home with the knife?"

"No." Two deep lines appeared between her eyes. Tears slid silently down her pale cheeks. She sniffled. "I don't."

"Mrs. Willager, has Viper Branch threatened you or your dog before?"

"Not directly, no. But the way he looks...looked... at my sweet girl sometimes, I got the message loud and clear. I know his history..."

She let the statement hang on the air between us, and Hal picked it up. "What *is* his history, Mrs. Willager?"

"He's killed animals before, Mr. Amity. Some proven, some just suspected. But Branch was a mean old soul. He was the consummate 'stay off my grass' grump. And his attitude always promised violence."

"But he'd never done anything violent to you in the past?"

She thought about it for a moment, her fingers twining rapidly. It was clear she knew something she didn't want to tell us.

I covered the twining fingers with my hand, stilling them. "What is it?" I asked gently.

Her lips compressed tightly and she gave her head a single, firm shake. "Viper Branch has never done anything overtly violent to my family or me."

Overtly? Was that a qualifier meant to obscure reality?

"Never?" Hal asked, disbelief coloring his softly-voiced question.

She shifted in her seat. "He and my husband used to have words, but it never came to violence."

Hal stared at his notes for a beat and then leaned

forward, clasping his hands in front of him and giving her a smile. "Mrs. Willager, do you believe Viper Branch poisoned Spunky?"

She twitched as he asked the question, her expression turning eminently sad. The twining fingers began to move again. Her chest heaved under labored breathing. "I believe it's possible. As I said, he has a history. And he definitely didn't like it when my girl walked onto his lawn. But I just don't know."

"Did Spunky go over there often?" I asked.

Mary shook her head. "I've trained her not to. That and the street. And as she's gotten older she just doesn't travel that much. She'll walk out to the big walnut tree in the front yard, and she usually lies down under that. But she doesn't...didn't...like Viper. She stayed away from him."

"Mrs. Willager," Hal asked. "If you had to guess someone who'd want to hurt your dog, who would it be?"

She didn't hesitate. "Nobody had a rational reason to hurt her, Mr. Amity. She's as sweet as they come. She doesn't hurt anybody."

"An irrational reason then?" he spurred.

Fresh tears filled her eyes. She sniffed, her hands finally stilling. "Then it would be Viper. He's the only one I can think of who might be able to convince himself she deserved it. Or who was evil enough to do it just because he could."

Hal thanked the older woman for her help and

walked with me to the door. We left after promising to have someone bring her some water.

Arno exited an unmarked door next to the interview room as Hal closed the door behind us. He motioned toward his office at the end of the hall.

We followed him into a good-sized office with a large window overlooking the highway.

Arno dropped heavily into his chair. He scrubbed a hand through his hair, looking ten years older than the last time I'd seen him. Then he sat forward, resting his elbows on his desk, and looked expectantly at Hal. "What do you think?"

"I'm not sure what to think," Hal responded after a moment. "The amnesia thing is strange."

Arno nodded. "I thought so too. If it was anybody else, I'd think she was lying."

"Maybe she is," Hal said, drawing a glower from Arno. Hal shrugged. "You asked me to help. I'm being honest with you, Arno. You've admitted you're too close to it to see things clearly."

Arno seemed to deflate.

"And she *is* lying," I said gently.

Arno turned his hostile gaze my way.

I shrugged. "I'm sorry, Arno. But when Hal asked her if Branch had ever been violent before, she was lying. I'd stake my whole property on it."

I thought, at first, that Arno was going to deny it. But after another significant pause, he sighed. "Your instincts are right, Joey. She wasn't lying exactly, but she wasn't telling the whole truth."

"What happened?" Hal asked, crossing his legs at the ankles and leaning back. The hard chair creaked under his weight.

Arno suddenly couldn't look at us. He stared hard at the pile of paperwork in the center of his desk. "I was ten. My dad had died that summer and Branch had grown increasingly mean-tempered as if he sensed we were vulnerable." Arno glanced up, his gaze finding mine and then sliding to Hal. "Viper Branch was a nasty piece of work. He'd always been foul. But when my dad was alive, he'd never crossed the line into threatening."

When Arno hesitated, Hal spurred him again. "But that changed when you were ten?"

Arno nodded. "I was playing ball with my friends. We were in the front yard, and the ball hit the big tree by the street and bounced into Branch's yard. I looked around first, to make sure he wasn't outside and then ran as fast as I could to get it." He stopped, frowning. "It was only a couple of feet over the line."

We waited for him to go on and, when he didn't, I said, "Did Branch confront you?"

"He..." Arno swallowed hard. "I'd just picked it up and turned back to my yard when I heard a shotgun being cocked."

I felt my eyes go wide. "He threatened you with a gun?"

Arno's frown deepened. "I almost peed myself. He told me if I ever stepped onto his lawn again, he'd shoot my mother first and then me."

Hal's hands fisted, and he sat forward. "I hope you went to the police?"

Arno didn't respond.

"Arno?" I asked gently.

"My mom didn't want to. She was too scared. She thought if we just stayed away from him, it would eventually blow over. I never played in my own yard again after that. It was another ten years before Mom even let herself get a dog. She was terrified he'd hurt it if it strayed."

"It looks like she was right," Hal offered.

Arno nodded. He finally glanced up. "She didn't want to tell you about it because she's ashamed. She feels guilty that she let Branch control our lives that way. She's gotten a lot stronger since then."

There was a beat of silence before Hal asked the question everybody in the room was thinking. "Strong enough to kill the man for harming her dog?"

Arno's gaze, when he glanced at us sparkled with unshed tears. "I just...don't know."

4

"*W*e need to talk to Reverend Smythe," I told Hal.

He nodded, pulling out of the lot for the Sherriff's Department on Highway 37 and heading north to Deer Hollow. "Do you want to grab some breakfast first?" he asked.

My stomach rumbled at his question. I glanced at the clock on the dash. "Sure. It's a little early to find the Reverend at the church. I think he usually gets in around nine."

Ten minutes later, Hal was pulling the SUV up in front of *Sonny's Diner*. He parked along the curb, and we climbed out.

Though the traffic through Deer Hollow had become a bit of a challenge as of late, due to the building of a new, giant subdivision south of town, the town was blessedly quiet.

More importantly, the diner was two-thirds empty, a circumstance that rarely happened since all the construction workers and electricians and plumbers had descended on our quiet little piece of country heaven like locusts.

A bell jingled softly as we entered the tatty country diner. Heading for the nearest booth, I scooted cautiously across the red vinyl seat, careful to avoid scraping my thighs on the curling red tape that held the battered vinyl together in the middle.

I looked around for the proprietress and chief waitress, Max, but she was nowhere to be found. I finally spotted her tangled yellow-blonde pile of hair through the order window. She was speaking to someone I couldn't see. Probably the cook.

Verna Bly moved slowly in our direction, her orthopedic shoes soundless on the old linoleum floor. She smiled as she placed a glass of water and a menu in front of us. "Mornin', folks. Coffee?"

Hal nodded. "Yes, please."

I shook my head, barely suppressing a grimace. The coffee at Sonny's was less like actual coffee and more like dirt-water run through old plumbing pipes in a truck stop bathroom.

"I'll just have some orange juice please."

Verna nodded briskly and left us to peruse the menu. My go-to-choice would have been biscuits drenched in sausage gravy with crispy bacon on the side. But I was currently dining with a Greek God who considered his body a temple. My body was a temple too. It was just a lazy temple filled with carbs, fat, and sugar and adorned with faded, fringed jean shorts, a cotton wife-beater tee with a picture of several Pitbulls and the caption, "Yes, I DO need this many Pitbulls," across the front, and cheap dime-store flipflops. My long blonde hair probably looked a wreck too. I hadn't taken the time to brush it before Hal and I flew out of my house in the middle of the night, simply pulling it back into a high pony and clamping its messy length with a hairband I happened to have around my wrist.

By stark contrast, even having been pulled into a murder investigation in the middle of the night, Hal's "temple" was impeccably covered in dark, un-creased jeans and a spotless white tee-shirt that fit him like a delicious cotton glove. He wore expensive-looking leather sandals on his feet, and there wasn't a strand out of place on his silky black hair.

I shoved self-consciously at some loose locks obscuring my view and looked at the egg-white omelet on the menu, wanting to cry.

I knew what I needed to do.

But that didn't mean I had to like it.

Verna returned with our drinks, settling them in front of us, and then pulled out her order pad, holding a pencil at the ready. She looked at me, but Hal spoke first.

"She'll have the biscuits and sausage gravy with

crispy bacon," he told Verna with a smile for me. "And I'll have the egg-white omelet, onion and green pepper, no cheese. Thanks!"

I wondered if he'd be embarrassed if I dropped to one knee on the linoleum and proposed on the spot. The whole Greek God package, along with an understanding of Bumpkin diet choices, made him almost too perfect for words.

Verna collected our menus and headed for the kitchen, calling it out to the cook in her husky voice as she dropped the menus back into the plastic holder on the back of the podium.

"I hope you don't mind my ordering for you," Hal said, his grin hidden as a kindness to me. All I saw when I looked at him was a neutral expression with a telltale spark of amusement in his green eyes.

I shrugged. "Actually, I was going to get the egg-white omelet," I told him, avoiding his gaze so he couldn't read the lie in my blue eyes.

"I can call her back and fix it," he teased.

"Don't you dare!" I said, slapping him on the hand.

He chuckled softly and the sound made my whole body warm, my stomach tightening with pleasure.

I sipped my juice, looking around and seeing no one I knew. There were a couple of men at a back booth. They were dressed in contractor-type cloth-ing, which included long jean-shorts, stained white tee-shirts, and heavy boots with work socks. Their hats bore the logos for their favorite sports teams rather than the easily recognizable John Deere logo. Even if I hadn't known they were outsiders, their caps would have clued me in fast.

"We should probably talk about our interview with Reverend Smythe," Hal said, sipping his coffee as I watched in fascination.

He grimaced but took another bite of the dirt-water before setting it down.

For a guy who tried to keep his body pure, nutritionally speaking, he sure was reckless with his coffee choices.

"We need to find out who was at that church meeting," I said, setting my juice back onto the table. "And figure out if anybody had it out for Mary Willager."

He nodded. "Or for Viper Branch."

I winced. "That's going to be pretty much everybody, I'm guessing."

"That's a strong possibility. But it's a place to start."

We sat back, falling silent as Verna placed our food in front of us.

I didn't speak for several minutes as I shoveled creamy, fatty goodness into my mouth. The only thing that would have made my breakfast more perfect would have been a short stack of Max's buttery pancakes.

But even a Bumpkin knew when not to push it with her perfect Greek God. I couldn't have Hal thinking I was a glutton. Though, the harsh truth was I could totally open my own branch office of Gluttons R Us.

"The Reverend might have some insight into how she was poisoned."

I blinked as I swallowed, thinking at first Hal meant Spunky. Then I realized he'd been talking about Mary. "You think somebody drugged Mrs. Willager?"

"Unless she has dementia, there's no other explanation for her not remembering what happened after she got home."

"Assuming she isn't lying."

Hal threw me a questioning look. "Do you believe her?"

I thought about it for a minute as I chewed and swallowed another delicious bite. I took a sip of juice and finally nodded. "I do. At least, I believe she *believes* she's telling the truth."

Hal swallowed and risked another bite of coffee. "We need to ask Arno if she could have dementia."

"He would have mentioned it, wouldn't he?"

"Normally, yes. But Arno's not thinking straight right now. He's an emotional wreck."

That was certainly the truth. "Doc Beetle might know."

Hal frowned. "Why would the veterinarian know

about a medical condition for one of the humans in town?"

"Because he's best friends with Doc Hamilton, the only people doctor in town." I grimaced. "I'm pretty sure they worked on Noah's Ark together."

Hal wiped his mouth, grinning as he settled his paper napkin into his empty plate. "Doc Hamilton's a bit old, you say?"

I grinned back. "He was old when the first settlers founded the colonies. He was already ancient when George Washington crossed the Delaware. I think he's even in the painting, handing George his daily dose of fiber."

Hal threw back his head and laughed. The sound made my whole body warm. "I love your version of history. If you'd been my history teacher in school, I'd have paid better attention."

Warmth infused my cheeks, no doubt turning my pale skin an embarrassing scarlet. "Most Deer Hollowans go to General Hospital outside of town for health care. There's a small practice of general practitioners there."

"But you think Mary goes to Doc Hamilton?"

I threw my napkin onto my empty plate. Although the word "empty" didn't quite cover it. My plate looked as if my pibl had licked it clean for me. I might have even scraped off some of the plate's shiny finish in my enthusiasm. "I don't *think*, I *know*. Arno too. They're both on the support local business bandwagon. Big time."

Hal picked up the check Verna had left at the edge of the table. "Ready?"

I made a play for the small piece of paper with Verna's unreadable scrawl on it. "I'll buy."

He jerked it away, sliding out of the booth and gliding gracefully toward the cash register by the door. "You leave the tip," he called back to me in his sexy voice.

I took a moment to stare at his lovely posterior features and then tugged my cell out of my shorts pocket, digging a five out of the phone wallet stuck to the side.

I caught up to him at the door and he opened it for me, allowing me to slip out ahead of him. But as I hit the sidewalk, I turned and wrapped myself around him before he knew what I was doing. I lifted onto my tippy toes as he smiled expectantly down at me. "Thanks for breakfast," I whispered before touching my lips to his.

When I broke the kiss, he licked his lips, a look of pure bliss crossing his handsome face. "Yum, you taste like bacon and gravy."

Waggling my eyebrows, I took his arm. "You're welcome. You can experience breakfast vicariously through me any time, Hal Amity."

The Lutheran Church sat at the very end of Main street in Deer Hollow, set back from the road on a grassy lot that housed a small cemetery on the east side. The west side encompassed a large parking lot, big enough to accommodate every person living in the Hollow and the surrounding countryside.

In the years since I'd been old enough to notice such things, I'd observed the parking lot had grown increasingly less crowded on Sundays. It was a trend that I knew had been playing out across the country...maybe around the world...as the place religion played in peoples' lives morphed due to cultural changes. It made me sad. Even though, as someone who'd stopped going to church after my parents had died, I was actually part of the problem.

Hal pulled his car into a parking spot in the nearly empty lot, and I made a promise to myself that I'd give serious thought to addressing my part in the sad change.

The rectory, otherwise known as Reverend Smythe's home, sat at the edge of the lot. The cozy little house was tucked partly behind the church and separated by a narrow strip of green grass and a row of rhododendron bushes Buck Mitzner of *Mitzner Landscaping* had recently donated to the church.

A small, puke-green car of some uninteresting make and model sat at the edge of the pavement in front of the rectory. "Should we check his house first?" I asked Hal, my gaze sliding over the boxy white clapboard home with a mud-brown roof.

Hal shook his head. "This time of day, he'll be in the sanctuary or his office."

I narrowed my gaze at my boyfriend. Hal had only recently semi-transplanted to Deer Hollow, yet he seemed to know the Rev's comings and goings better than I did. "And you know this, how?"

Hal gave me an enigmatic smile. "The pastor told me once."

We headed for the double front doors of the old-fashioned white country church. It looked like a thousand other country churches, with a pretty spire towering into the clear blue sky and pale wood doors framed by slim windows filled with stained glass depicting angels and stuff.

I'd never studied the depictions all that carefully because angels had always scared the snot out of me. I believe it has something to do with the fierce looks on their faces.

There didn't seem to be a lot of wiggle room in the way they viewed right and wrong. Plus, there was the wing thing. When I thought about all-powerful creatures flying over the Earth watching my every move, I felt a little like a field mouse with hawks circling overhead.

Hal pulled the door open for me, and I scurried

through ahead of him, my gaze deliberately avoiding the scowling angels in the glass.

We walked through the hushed entranceway. The lobby was pleasantly infused with the sweet scent of flowers, courtesy of a giant bouquet sitting on a highly-polished wood table in the center of the space.

The doors to the sanctuary were open and a man stood on the steps leading to the altar. His shoulders were slightly rounded, and his dark head was bowed in prayer.

I stopped when I saw him, not wanting to interrupt. Reverend Smythe seemed to sense our presence and turned, smiling when he saw us standing near the door. "Joey, Hal, welcome." He motioned with one hand. "Come, come."

We moved forward, and unease filled me as I walked up the aisle to the waiting pastor. It had been a long time since I'd entered the heavy silence of the church and, though the atmosphere was soothing, I couldn't shake the feeling that I didn't quite belong there anymore.

Reverend Smythe took Hal's hand, giving it a firm shake before reaching for mine. "It's so good to see you here again, Joey."

My cheeks heated and I looked away, avoiding Hal's gaze. For some reason, I didn't want him to know that I'd been remiss in my religiosity. Not that I thought he would judge me. Hal never seemed to do that. I guessed I just wanted him to admire me in all things. "I'm happy to be here," I finally said, lamely.

The pastor nodded, crossing his hands in front of him and looking back and forth between us. "You need my help with something."

It wasn't a question. He saw the truth in our expressions. He seemed only mildly disappointed that we weren't there for more spiritual reasons. "What can I do for you?"

"You heard about Viper Branch?" Hal asked the pastor.

Reverend Smythe nodded, frowning. "Terrible thing."

He looked at me and I nodded too, though I'd never met the infamous Mr. Branch and probably would have hated him if I had. "I'm sure you know that Mary Willager's been arrested for his murder?"

Reverend Smythe sighed. "Just horrible. I've been to the station to pray with her."

"Is Arno still keeping her in an interview room?" I asked.

"His office, I believe. He's made up the couch for her."

Of course he had. I nodded. "He's not dealing very well with all this."

"I'm not sure how you deal well with the knowledge that your mother killed someone," the pastor offered.

"Do you believe she did it?" Hal asked.

"Killed Branch? I certainly don't want to believe it." He shook his head. "But, you know how it is, Mr. Amity. When you've known someone for most of your life, it's sometimes hard to recognize what they're capable of."

"You believe Mary is capable of taking a knife and stabbing a man to death with it?" I couldn't help asking. I felt a little betrayed that the pastor didn't at least keep an open mind about her innocence.

"I didn't say that, Joey. It's just..."

"You know how much she loves Spunky," Hal offered.

"Yes. And, though I hate to speak ill of the dead, Mr. Branch was a singularly unpleasant creature. I doubt there's a person in Deer Hollow who hasn't considered running him over with a car at least once."

I barked out a laugh. "Does that include you, Reverend?" To my surprise, he hesitated.

When he finally spoke, his words shocked me. "I once saw him try to run over a kitten in the street. He veered right for it, laughing as he did. Fortunately, he missed. But I snatched up that kitten and brought her home, just in case." He smiled widely. "Her name's Willow."

"You still have her," I asked, surprised.

"I do. The Lord saved her from that horrible man right in front of me. I recognize a message from God when I see it, young lady. She's been a wonderful companion for me for several years now."

"Mary doesn't remember what happened that night," Hal told him. "Can you think of any reason for that?"

Reverend Smythe held Hal's gaze for a long moment before responding. Then he frowned. "What exactly are you asking me, son?"

"We know she was here right before it happened."

The pastor nodded. "A meeting of the flower committee." He motioned toward the beautiful display in the entrance. "Mary designed that herself. She was very talented with flowers."

His words reminded me that Mary had once owned a flower shop on Main Street. It had closed when she retired.

"Did she eat or drink anything while she was here?" Hal asked.

Reverend Smythe stared thoughtfully into the distance for a moment. "I believe they had tea and cookies. That's usually what they have at those meetings."

"Can you show us?" Hal asked.

"Of course. They hold their meetings at the big table in the kitchen. It's downstairs. Follow me."

As we headed down the stairs, which were located off to the side of the front doors, Hal asked about the members of the flower committee.

"Just the usual people," the pastor told him. "Nancy Villa, Verna Gregg, and Old Mrs. Watson, though I'm pretty sure she only comes for the cookies." He laughed. "Oh, and a new woman who just joined the committee recently." He tapped a finger on his chin. "What was her name? Oh yes, Samantha Powers. She was one of the first to move into the new Hollows subdivision. She's a very nice woman."

He stopped in the doorway to a good-sized kitchen, swinging an arm toward an assortment of outdated appliances and a haphazard array of painted and chipped cabinets that were probably as old as the hundred-year-old church. Situated in the center of the space was an old, Formica-topped table and a mismatched assortment of chairs. "You're welcome to anything here. I believe they had some of the cookies left. And the tea is in that big cookie jar there on the counter. The one that looks like a pig." He smiled fondly around the room. Clearly, the pastor didn't see old and outdated when he looked at the church kitchen. He appeared to love every inch of the place.

"If you don't mind, I'd like to bag the stuff up and take it in for Deputy Willager to send to the lab."

"You think Mary was drugged?" the Reverend asked astutely.

"It's possible. There could only be a couple of reasons for her to forget whole chunks of time."

"I'm sure the emotional trauma of finding her

poor dog like that and then killing another human might be enough to do it," Reverend Smythe said, his tone slightly chastising.

Hal simply inclined his head. It was clear the reverend didn't like having his flower committee besmirched.

"Do you know if Mary could have dementia," I offered to distract him from Hal moving around the kitchen to gather the items to be tested.

"Dementia? Why, I don't know. If she did, she hid it well."

"Memory issues are a big part of the disease," I told him. I'd once dated a guy whose father had early-onset dementia, and the poor man would forget things from one minute to the next. "It's a horrible disease. But patients can seem perfectly normal one minute and then forget everything they'd done five minutes earlier in the next."

He nodded. "Yes. I've dealt with it in the church." He thought about my question for a moment and then nodded. "It's possible. I only saw Mary for short periods of time and only a couple of times a week. She could have hidden her condition."

"But you've never spoken about it with her," I asked, just to clarify.

"No. You should ask her physician." Then he caught himself. "But he wouldn't tell you, would he?" Reverend Smythe shook his head. "I'm sorry I couldn't be more helpful."

"You've been very helpful, Reverend. Arno will appreciate your being so open with us."

"I'm glad to help." He looked at his watch. "Now, if you'll excuse me, I've procrastinated enough. I need to get busy writing this week's sermon. You can see yourselves out?"

I assured him we could and watched him walk slowly back toward the stairs. His step seemed heavier than usual. I realized the whole murder thing, and Mary's subsequent arrest probably weighed heavily on him.

But as he slid a glance back my way, an unhappy expression on his lined face, I couldn't help wondering if there wasn't something more weighing him down.

Had he told us everything he knew?

5

---

*C*aphy was whining when we came out of the police station. She was probably thirsty and needed to go potty. I was just about to tell Hal to take us home when my phone rang. Looking at caller ID, I realized it was Arno. He'd been in his boss's office when we'd come in, so we hadn't had a chance to talk to him. "Hey, Arno. We just dropped some stuff off with a Deputy Craig to be tested."

"Yeah, I just spoke to him. He said it came from the church? What's that about?"

"I'm putting you on speaker," I told Arno. "Hal's here with me now."

"Hey," Arno said, sounding tired.

"Hey, Arno," Hal responded. "We found out that your mom had been at a flower committee meeting at the Lutheran church before she came home last night. We thought if she'd been drugged, that would be the most logical place for it to have happened."

"Wait," Arno paused, and I could picture him scrubbing a hand over his weary eyes. "Drugged?"

"She said she can't remember why she was standing over Branch with that knife," I told him gently. "Can you think of any other reason why she might have blacked out like that?"

A silence pulsed down the phone line, and Hal and I shared a look. Finally, Arno said. "You're going with the idea that my mother did kill Branch but she just can't remember it?"

I realized too late how Arno would take what we were asking him.

I was glad when Hal spoke up so I didn't have to. "Arno, we're not assuming anything at this point. Maybe the killer drugged her so she'd forget seeing him kill Branch. But it's a thread we need to follow. You know it's true."

Arno sighed. "Yeah. I do. This just..."

"Sucks," I said for him. "We understand. Just try to keep the positive thought."

Hal took a moment to explain what we'd collected and discuss the other women at the committee.

I sat there, dreading my next question.

"I'm aware that Verna's husband had some kind of disagreement with Branch last month," Arno told us. "The two of them broke up Mable's Bar out on Buck Hollow road."

"Do you have any idea what the fight was about?" Hal asked.

"Not really. They were both drunk as skunks. I'm not sure *they* even knew what they were fighting about."

"Okay, we'll go talk to him."

Hal looked at me, lifting his brows. I'd been squirming and chewing on my bottom lip throughout their conversation.

I took a deep breath. "Uh, Arno?"

"I need to get going, Joey. What is it?"

I glanced one more time at Hal and he gave me an encouraging smile. I'm thinking he'd guessed what I was trying to work up the courage to ask.

"I...uh..."

"Joey, can this wait?"

"Does your mother have dementia?" As soon as the words spewed from between my lips—ugly and feral things that spilled tension through the air like toxic gas—I dropped my head into my hands.

Hal reached out and squeezed my arm in support. But Arno was quiet for so long I thought he'd hung up on us.

Finally, I heard a sigh. "Not that I know of. For sure, anyway."

That was a lot of qualifiers for such a short

response. "For sure?" I spurred, hoping he'd elaborate.

"I have to go." He hung up before I could stop him.

I looked at Hal. "What do you think of that?"

"I think Arno knows she has dementia and doesn't want to face it."

I nodded, agreeing.

"Shall we go talk to Verna's husband?"

Out of the frying pan and right into the dang fire. "Yeah. I guess we should."

Verna and Robert Bly lived in one of the newer subdivisions on the western fringe of Deer Hollow. The house was red-gray brick on the front, with tan siding on the sides and back. The two-door garage was opened up to the soft breezes running across the subdivision, no doubt originating from the Fawn River, which hugged the western edge of town and jutted around the southern tip for a half mile before straightening out again and flowing toward Indianapolis.

Robert Bly was bent over one of his beloved antique cars in one bay of the garage, his white tee-shirt stained with grease and stretched out of shape at the front neckline where he was no doubt using it to mop sweat off his cadaverous face.

He looked up when Hal drove his SUV onto the short concrete drive and grabbed the rag he'd draped over the car as he worked, using it to clean oil from his hands as he approached the Escalade.

Bly slid a wary gaze over Hal before looking at me. His bony face transformed under a wide smile. "Joey. How are you?"

I waved. "Hey, Robert. This is my friend Hal."

Hal shook Robert's hand without even flinching. Since I was pretty sure it involved the transposing of a lot of grease and oil, I was impressed by his lack of concern. "Mr. Bly. It's a pleasure." Hal jerked his head toward the dismembered antique in the garage. "Is that a 1963 Corvette?"

Robert's face flared to life, his fleshless features transforming as he grinned widely. "Are you a car aficionado?"

Hal crossed his arms over his chest, eyeing the dismembered vehicular cadaver with something that looked surprisingly like longing. "Only of Corvettes. The 63 was my first car. I named her Grace. She was particular and sometimes resistant to my affections. But I never felt less than blessed when I was wrapped in her loving embrace."

I fought the impulse to gag.

Robert Bly laughed knowingly. "Found this one at Parson's last summer. I've been replacing her parts as I locate them."

Hal nodded. "Lucky man."

I wasn't entirely certain, but I thought Parson's was a huge junkyard between Deer Hollow and Indy.

Clearly feeling pretty good about life at the moment, Robert Bly cast his happy gaze my way. "If you're looking for Verna, she's still over at the diner."

I shook my head, regretting that our reason for being there was probably going to ruin his good mood. "No, we actually needed to speak with you."

His oversized eyes, such a dark brown that they looked black, widened with curiosity. "Oh? What about?" Then he got a sly look. "Wait, is this about the wrapping paper fundraiser? 'Cause I bought fifty dollars worth last spring and we haven't used it all up yet. I'm all for supporting the girls' soccer team, but I can't help them out this year, I'm afraid." He lifted his hands in support of his obvious regret. "I'm sorry, Joey."

"Thank you for your support on that. I'm happy to say the High School has decided the girls deserve their encouragement and they're buying the uniforms this year."

"Oh, that's good," he said, his smile twitching briefly back into place. Bly narrowed his gaze. "So, what is this about, then?"

"We wanted to ask you about Viper Branch," Hal told the other man.

Robert frowned, his lips opening in surprise. He seemed genuinely perplexed for a moment, and then his expression cleared. "Ah, you're investigating Branch's murder." Amazingly, Bly laughed, shaking his head as he planted bony hands on his narrow hips. "I'm just remembering that you're a private investigator, Hal."

Hal nodded. "I am, sir."

"We're helping Arno, Robert," I said gently. "You can imagine how this has upset him."

My cynical ploy to gain Robert's sympathy worked. If I could keep him from getting angry with us for basically asking him if he'd killed Branch, things would go much smoother.

"I heard Mary Willager was found standing over that SOB with a knife." Robert shook his head. "I would have never thought she had it in her. Lord knows we've all been there. But nobody's had the guts to remove that demon from the world until now."

"You believe Mary Willager killed Viper Branch?" Hal asked.

Bly hesitated. "Not really, no. But they caught her with the knife, right?"

Hal didn't answer Robert's question. "Why would Mary have wanted Branch dead?"

Bly blew a raspberry. "Why *wouldn't* she have? The man was so evil he left a trail of sulfur behind when he moved. I believe any of us could have killed him under the right circumstances."

"Even you?" I asked.

Bly didn't even hesitate. "Absolutely. I don't mind telling you that I hated that man with a passion."

"Did you kill him?" Hal asked softly.

Bly looked from Hal to me and then back again. "You're serious?"

Hal inclined his head. "As you said, lots of people in town had motive to do it. Our job is to find out who had opportunity too."

"I was here all night."

"Can anybody vouch for you?" Hal asked.

"My wife." Even as he said it, Bly seemed to realize how weak it was. Especially since he'd just admitted he'd have killed Viper Branch himself under the right circumstances. He flushed a deep red, and his lips tightened. "I didn't kill the man."

"We understand you fought with Branch last month."

Bly's mouth fell open, and some of the blood that had just rushed to his head fled again, leaving him a pale shade of red rather than the burgundy color he'd been a moment earlier. "Who told you that?"

"Robert, we did tell you that we were helping Arno out on this case, right?" I reminded him.

He sighed, looked down at the ground, and shook his head. "You should just ask Arno. It's all in the police report. Branch and I both spent the night in a cell."

"We're asking you," Hal said, his voice firm.

"It wasn't anything important."

"Let us decide that, please, Mr. Bly." Hal was working hard to keep just the right tone that rode the razor's edge between uncompromising and understanding.

"The man parked too close to me at Mable's. When he got out of his Jeep, he smashed the door into my car." Bly met Hal's gaze. "It was a 1973 Mustang convertible. She was in pristine condition. And Branch deliberately took a chunk out of her." When he saw the right amount of disgust reflected in Hal's gaze, Bly nodded. "He didn't even try to deny it. The man was Satan himself. I'm not surprised somebody killed him. I'm just surprised it didn't happen a long time ago."

We decided to stop by the scene of the crime on the way home. As we drove up the quiet residential street, I was struck by how quiet and serene it was in the light of day, without a bunch of Sheriff's cars with lights flaring over the landscape and no dead body whose deeply flawed soul had probably been pulled directly south into the fiery pits.

We drove under an overarching array of enormous trees that kept the sun at bay and dropped the temp in Hal's car by several degrees. Caphy's nose was pressed against the glass as we neared the end of the street. She was no doubt looking for her friend Spunky in the quiet neighborhood.

Hal parked in the well-tracked grass where all the Sherriff's cars had parked the night before. We climbed out, and I let Caphy out too. She ran directly to the spot where Spunky had been lying, sniffing the ground carefully around the area.

I realized Spunky might have vomited in the grass and hurried over to grab Caphy by the collar, leading her safely away before letting her go again. She ran over to the scruffy patch of lawn in front of Branch's double-wide and squatted, peeing happily on a tall weed there.

I smiled, feeling a certain sense of karma that my dog was peeing on Satan's lawn and there was nothing he could do about it.

Hal came up next to me, jerking his head toward the house on the other side of Branch. "We should talk to the neighbors."

I frowned. "Didn't the deputies talk to them last night?"

"They did. But I'm thinking people might tell us a bit more than they would someone in a uniform."

He was right. Especially in a small country town, people spoke more freely to someone they considered part of their "group" than they did someone who had the power to drag them into the station and throw them into a cell.

"We should downplay the 'helping Arno' thing then," I told him. He nodded. "I'll let you take the lead."

I grinned, happy that he trusted me with the interview. Then I realized that what I was about to attempt was basically little more than indulge in helpful gossip. That took me down a notch.

The red brick home next to Viper Branch's property was the biggest home on the street. It was set further back from the road than everybody else too, with a good three acres of perfectly manicured lawn as a buffer to the street and a wooden privacy fence running along the property line between the neighbor's acreage and Branch's lawn. The privacy fence ran all the way to the street, forcing us to walk along Antler's Way to the driveway and then trek up the winding asphalt to the big house.

A well-padded woman in a wide-brimmed straw hat was bent over an unruly flowering bush near the house. The bush was beautiful, heavy with large-petaled pink flowers and almost as tall as she was. The woman didn't seem to hear our approach and only looked up when Hal called out.

"Hello!"

The gardening homeowner turned to look at us. Unfortunately, her wide-brimmed hat stuck on her oversized shirt and didn't turn with her. She found herself staring into what was probably sweat-drenched straw and plucked the hat away with a giggle as she slowly straightened, groaning and clutching her lower back as she rose.

"This isn't getting any easier with age," she shouted, smiling at us as we stopped in front of her.

"Hello. I'm Joey and this is Hal…" I said.

The woman frowned and then shook her head. "I can't hear you," she shouted back, pointing to her ears. She spotted Caphy and smiled widely. "Well, hello, pretty girl," she screamed. My startled pibl dove behind my legs as the woman tried to pet her.

"This is Caphy," I shouted.

The woman's frown had me panicking. She was clearly deaf as a post. It was beginning to look like we might have to resort to primal screams to inter-view her.

Suddenly her face cleared and she laughed again, reaching to pluck a small black object from one ear and then the other. "Sorry. Earbuds. I forgot I was wearing them. I'm listening to an audiobook." She flushed with embarrassment.

A distant voice emerged from the buds as she dropped them into a big pocket in what I could now see was a gardening smock with oversized compart-ments. She started to offer me her hand and then stopped, laughing once more as she tugged the filthy glove from her fingers. "I'm Ginnie," she told us. "And you are?"

I took her hand, finding it moist and a little gritty. "I'm Joey. This is my friend Hal. We're helping Mary Willager."

The woman's ruddy face folded into a frown. "Ah, poor Mary. I just can't believe she's being blamed for that monster's death."

Okay then. No questions regarding how she felt about Viper Branch would be necessary.

"You don't believe she did it?" Hal asked.

"Of course not." The woman's hazel gaze sharpened as she looked him over. "I presume you know Mary. Do you believe she killed that man?"

"Everybody we talk to says the whole town hated him," I offered.

Ginnie nodded enthusiastically. "That's the God's honest truth. The man seemed to go out of his way to be hateful."

Caphy wandered over and carefully sniffed the pocket of Ginnie's smock. She reached down and scratched behind the pibl's ears, earning herself a lifelong friend. Caphy dropped to her butt in the grass and pressed into the scratching fingers, getting a hearty chuckle from her new friend.

"Did you see anything last night, Ginnie?" Hal asked. "Anything that would help Mary," he wisely added.

She scanned a glance toward Mary's house,

though it was largely hidden by the fence, Branch's trailer, and the trees. "Mary left at the usual time for her meeting at the church."

"How about before she left?" Hal asked. "Did anyone stop by?"

Ginnie squinted her eyes. I realized after a moment that she was thinking. "Not that I can remember, no."

"While she was at church, did anyone come to her house?" I asked.

Ginnie's eyes widened, and she nodded. "Now that you mention it, she did get a visit from Nancy Villa while she was out. That isn't unusual at all. Nancy always brought Mary fresh eggs."

I tucked that little tidbit away to talk to Lis about. I hadn't been aware that Mrs. Villa raised chickens.

"What time did she arrive?" Hal asked.

"Oh, I'm guessing it was a little after five pm. I remember thinking it was strange she came then because she knew Mary always had her flower committee meeting at five. She generally left ten minutes before five on the dot."

"Did you speak to Mrs. Villa?" Hal asked.

I was struck silent as Nancy Villa fell unexpectedly into a suspect slot. She was my best friend's mom. I'd known the woman all my life, had considered her a second mom when I was growing up. If Nancy started to look guilty, I was quickly going to find myself in the same boat as Arno.

Ginnie shook her head. "No. But I was working on the flowers around the mailbox down by the road and I saw her car cruise by."

Hal nodded. "What about Mr. Branch? Did he get any other visitors last night?"

The woman blew air through her lips. "Branch rarely got visitors. He generally met everyone who dared to step onto his property with a shotgun." She shook her head. "Only exception was that lawyer fella. The mean one. Those two were peas in a pod."

My enforced silence broke at her words, and my pulse spiked. "You mean George Shulz?"

Ginnie's lips curled. "That's the fella. I don't know why anybody would work with him if they didn't have to. He's a real tool."

I couldn't help nodding my agreement. Hal and I had crossed paths with Shulz before. He was indeed a tool.

And many worse things.

"Do you know why Branch was spending time with Shulz?" Hal asked.

"No clue. But whatever it was, they had meetings every week like clockwork."

"Shulz came to Branch's home every week?" Hal asked, frowning.

"Yep. Strangest thing. Far as I know, the lawyer never leaves that disgusting office except when he has to go to court. But I'm guessing he came here because he didn't want Branch killing off his cats." She shook her head in disgust.

Hal offered her his hand and she took it, smiling. "Thank you so much, Ginnie. You've been a lot of help."

"I'm glad to help. Mary is the sweetest thing. Anything I can do to help her, I want to do."

"Then you won't mind if we come back," I asked, trying to look harmless. "If we think of more questions."

She took my hand too, giving it a squeeze instead of a shake. "You're welcome here any time, Joey." Her expression turned sad. "I'm so sorry about your parents, hon. That had to have been just awful for you."

I clutched my happy secret close and nodded. The truth was, I'd recently learned that my mom hadn't been on the plane that crashed. But for reasons of her safety, I couldn't tell anybody that. I was just glad Hal and Arno knew so I didn't have to lie to them.

Unfortunately, my dad hadn't been so lucky.

"Thank you so much. It's been hard." I glanced down at Caphy, tears swimming in my eyes as I found her looking expectantly at me. It was like she understood what we were talking about. "Caphy saved me. She pulled me through it when I thought I'd never be able to function normally again."

Ginnie nodded. "I understand. My Thelma was like that. I miss her so much."

"Was that your dog?" Hal asked gently.

"A Chihuahua Pekinese mix. Such a pretty girl. And she made me smile just by being there. She was the only thing that kept me going when I lost my husband."

I took Ginnie's chubby fingers into my hand and squeezed them. "I'm so sorry. When did you lose her?"

Ginnie sniffed, her cheeks wet with new tears. "Six months ago." She brushed the back of her hand under her eyes, leaving behind a streak of dirt. "I miss her as much now as I did right after it happened."

"If you don't mind my asking, how did it happen?"

Ginnie shrugged. "She was in the house with me. She was hiding from the vacuum. She always hated the sound of the vacuum," Ginnie shared tearfully. "I heard the slam of the front door and turned off the vacuum. I hadn't been expecting anyone. Next thing I know, I hear squealing tires, and I just knew somehow." She sniffled, her eyes red.

"I'm so sorry," I repeated, at a loss. But a sudden thought was rearing its ugly head. "Was it Branch?" I asked the distraught woman? "Did he hit her with his car?"

She sniffled. "No. I'd love to blame him. But it

wasn't Branch. I'm afraid it was poor Nancy. She was so upset." Ginnie sobbed softly. "I never blamed her. It wasn't her fault my Thelma ran in front of her car." She shook her head again. "It really wasn't her fault."

I couldn't help wondering if Ginnie was trying to convince us of that...or herself.

6

"*L*unch, Nancy Villa or George Shulz?"

I didn't bother hiding a wince. "I can't accuse Lis's mom of murdering Viper Branch on an empty stomach." Actually, I was pretty sure I couldn't do it on a full stomach either. But I'd cross that wobbly bridge hanging high above a crocodile-laden river with deadly rapids later.

Hal reached across the car and patted my knee. "Lunch it is. How about we take a walk on the wild side and have tacos?"

I perked up considerably, unable to believe he was even suggesting it. "What about the temple?"

"Macho Taco has a new fish taco I've been meaning to try."

I grimaced. "Yuck! That sounds nasty."

"Is that a no on Macho Taco then?"

"Absolutely not! They have a Mondo Meat Burrito *I've* been meaning to try."

"Macho Taco it is, then." Hal turned on Duck Waddle Road and headed for the small building near the river. Macho Menendez had opened the taco joint after the Coffee Beanery had failed spectacularly in that spot. The 400 square foot building with a drive-through window hadn't pulled in enough coffee consumers to support its modest expenses. I was no business expert, but I figured it had been due to the fact that the coffee had usually been cold and the service had ranged from slow to glacial.

But where the residents of Deer Hollow weren't ready to drop three dollars for a burnt-tasting cup of cold joe—even when partially masked by chocolate syrup and fluffy mounds of whipped cream—we were more than willing to stand and drive in lines to stuff our gullets with sloppy burritos and messy beef, chicken or pulled pork tacos.

What could I say? Most of us cut our teeth on politically incorrect comfort food riddled with carbs and calories. Proving, Hal's fish tacos aside, that country folk had better taste in food than city folk.

We eschewed the drive-through, which at five minutes to noon was already half a block long, and parked in the restaurant's small lot. I staked out a table with only moderate bird poopage and Hal headed to the window to purchase our food.

After de-pooping the table with napkins from Hal's car, I dumped the trash in the nearby trash receptacle and sat down to people watch. The line at the walk-up window wasn't much better than the drive-through. Hal had only moved the distance of three people when a familiar voice hailed me from a car in the drive-through.

I looked up and grinned when I saw my best friend Lis waving at me. A moment later, she veered her car out of the line and drove around, parking the sexy, low-slung sports car in the spot next to Hal's car.

I stood up and hugged her as she joined me, a wide grin on her stunning face. "I didn't know you were going to be in town. Why didn't you call me?" I scolded happily.

"I just drove in," she explained, waving at Hal over my head. He pointed to the menu and she called out, "fish tacos and a water."

I grimaced. "Et tu, Brutus?"

Lis giggled. "Sorry. The tacos aren't exactly good for my next swimwear shoot, but I figure if they're fish, I can sort of justify it."

My gorgeous, statuesque friend was a semi-famous magazine model who was gone from Deer Hollow more than she was there. We'd been friends since grade school, and I loved her like a sister. It was always fun to see her. "I hope your mom's okay?"

She gave me a look as she slid her long legs over

the hard-plastic bench. "She's fine. Can't I just come home because I'm homesick?"

"Absolutely." I gave her another impulsive hug. Then the smile slid from my face. "You heard about Mary Willager?"

Lis shook her head, frowning. "Oh no, don't tell me she's..."

"Not gone, no." I gave her an apologetic look. "But almost as bad. She was found standing over Viper Branch with a bloody knife."

Lis sucked air, covering her mouth with a perfectly manicured hand. I fought the urge to hide my own, unpainted, slightly dry hands with tattered nails in my lap. "Poor Arno!"

"Yeah. As you can imagine, he's not taking it well."

"Is Mary locked up?"

"Sort of. She's actually sleeping in Arno's office."

Lis lifted her stunningly microbladed brows and I nodded. "I told you he was a mess."

"I should stop by and see her...him...them."

"That would be great." An awkward silence fell between us as I struggled with how to ask Lis about her mom and the eggs. Finally, I settled for a slightly less volatile subject. "Arno asked Hal and me to investigate the murder for him, since he's way too close to it."

She frowned. "Aren't there other deputies who could do it? Or even someone from Indy?"

"Oh yeah. But Arno doesn't trust an outsider to do this. His mother's life depends on what we turn up. And..." I leaned close. "To tell you the truth, it doesn't look good for Mary."

Lis's eyes widened again. "You really think she killed that Branch guy?"

"Apparently, the townies all hate him. He sounds like a real piece of work."

She nodded, glancing up as Hal arrived, laden with three plastic baskets and three bottles of water.

"Thanks so much, Hal," Lis said, giving him a wide grin. "I've been dreaming about these tacos for a week."

"My pleasure," he said, winking at me. I felt a warm glow as his muscular thigh met mine on the bench. It was inevitable that I'd suffer a bit from jealousy of my gorgeous friend. Once or twice I'd even convinced myself that Hal might prefer Lis's statuesque, classic beauty over my own, comfortable, girl-next-door prettiness. But I'd gotten over those insecurities as Hal and I had grown closer.

Mostly.

I felt a sudden and surprising surge of compassion for Lis. In her job, she had to watch every bite she put in her mouth. It had to be a tough way to live. Personally, if I tried to live under her regimen, it wouldn't survive my first encounter with banana cream pie.

I grabbed a plastic fork and knife from the pile

Hal had placed in the middle of the table, slicing off a bite of burrito. "And to answer your question, no, I don't believe Mary did it. But I care about her and Arno. If I was just trying to close a case, I might not be so open-minded."

Lis shook her head. "Still...I can't believe Sheriff Mulhern would let Arno delegate it to a couple of civilians."

Hal swallowed a bite of taco. "Arno actually deputized me before we started."

I glanced his way, startled. I hadn't known.

Hal shrugged. "I was a cop in Indianapolis for a decade. I'm a licensed investigator. It isn't a totally random idea."

Lis nodded. Then she gave me a sideways glance, grinning wickedly. "And Joey's qualifications are what? Most experienced at finding dead bodies?"

"Har, Miss Lis. That isn't actually a bad qualification. I do have lots of experience with the life-challenged."

She snorted, spitting water across the table. "Life challenged?"

I grinned back.

"No. Joey's my civilian consultant. She knows all the people and helps me navigate the socio-political climate in Deer Hollow."

"That sounds like a business proposal," Lis joked.

"Not far from it. If the Sheriff demands justification for our work, I'm ready to give it to him."

We chewed in silence for a few minutes. I ate my burrito, trying to focus on the happy thought that I was sitting with my two favorite people in the world, enjoying a sunny day in the cool shade, with the pleasing view and familiar scent of the Fawn River as a backdrop. Adding to the pleasant scene was the happy chirp of voices around us, and the sweet scent of flowers coming from the beds around the restaurant.

Hal and Lis seemed perfectly happy. But then Hal didn't have the same connection to Lis and her mom that I did. And Lis was happily ignorant of the trauma I was about to invoke in her world.

I was so upset, in fact, that I only managed to eat two-thirds of my burrito before the bites got caught in my clenched throat.

Okay, fifteen-sixteenths of my burrito.

All right! I left one bite in the basket. Are you happy now?

I dropped my fork onto the waxed paper lining my basket and pushed it away. "Lis..."

Hal's head came up, his gaze catching mine. I wasn't sure if his green gaze was shooting a warning my way or sympathy.

It didn't really matter. I had to do what I was about to do.

Still, I surprised everyone at the table with my

starting point. "I didn't know your mom was raising chickens."

Lis blinked, looking surprised by my statement. "Chickens? Is that a joke?"

I shook my head, using my paper napkin to brush food debris off the table into my hand. "Not according to one of Mary's neighbors. She said your mom brought fresh eggs to Mary once a week. Like clockwork."

Lis thought about it for a moment, then seemed to have a lightbulb moment. "Ah, yes. You're right. She and Aunt Betty are raising them at my Aunt Betty's farm. I'd forgotten about it." She popped the last bite of taco into her mouth and sat back, chewing around a grin.

"Why?" I asked. The question didn't necessarily have anything to do with the case we were working on. But I was curious.

Lis shrugged. "Who knows? Aunt Betty has always been able to talk my mom into stupid stuff. When they were kids, she talked her into taunting a Brahma bull her daddy kept on the farm." She shook her head. "I almost wasn't born."

"Yikes!" I laughed, kind of relieved that there was a simple and probably silly reason for the chickens.

"I'm guessing they were just looking for a little extra spending money. I think they've also experimented with honey making, but I don't think that went anywhere." She grimaced. "I remember having to clean out the chicken coop when I was around eight years old. Nasty business."

I'd put more stock in that if Lis didn't believe any kind of manual labor with the potential to get dirty was nasty.

She sipped her water, staring out at the sparkling surface of the river for a moment before she seemed to grow very still, turning to me. "I'm so stupid."

"What?" I was relaxed, enjoying a gentle breeze that cooled the sweat from my brow and thinking my best friend was about to admit to some knowledge she hadn't known she possessed. My metaphorical underbelly was exposed, pale and flabby, when she hit me.

Not real hitting, of course. That might bruise her million-dollar knuckles.

"You think my mom killed that guy."

I looked into her stunned expression, the hurt-filled eyes like blades driving right into my heart. I was so shocked by her accusation that my mind blanked.

Totally. Blanked.

Hal to the rescue. "We don't think anything of the kind, Lis." His tone was soft, but firm. "You know we have to follow up on information we're given. We didn't solicit this information. But now that it's been given to us we need to ask the questions."

Lis turned a stony gaze to Hal. "You're going to ask my mother if she killed Viper Branch?"

"No!" I managed to choke out. Thank goodness I was able to add so much to the conversation.

"We're going to ask her if she saw anybody who might have been responsible when she was there," Hal responded. "We're going to ask her if anything seemed out of the ordinary." He leaned closer, his voice lowering. "And, yes, we're going to ask her if she had any reason to dislike the victim. We'd be failing in our job here if we didn't."

Lis surged to her feet. "Job? You haven't been hired, Hal Amity. You've been coerced into trying to save Arno's butt." She turned to me, her gaze blazing. "And you..." She poked her finger in my direction. "You aren't trained to investigate anything. You're both a couple of hacks, just trying to take the pressure off Mary Willager. Shame on you," she said to me as tears slipped down my cheeks. "Shame on both of you!" she stalked away, sliding into her sexy little car and slamming the door before laying rubber on the lot and roaring away.

I stared after her, feeling as if my heart was breaking.

Hal reached over and placed a hand on my arm, giving it a squeeze.

But I didn't want his pity. I didn't want to be comforted. Lis was right. I was a fraud. And my bumbling around pretending to be Sherlock Holmes just might have lost me my best friend.

7

"*D*o you want to wait out here?" Hal asked me when he parked in front of Nancy's Villa's tidy brick home.

I stared at the small front porch, painted white like the rest of the trim, and remembered all the balmy summer nights Lis and I had spent sucking on cherry-flavored popsicles there. I didn't *want* to go inside. But I knew I should. "I'll come."

Nancy didn't answer the door when we knocked. I suffered a horrifying flash of self-doubt that she knew why we were there and already hated me.

But then we heard the strident clang of something against metal and realized she must be in the back yard.

We descended the porch steps and headed around to the back, following a sidewalk that rolled like the ocean over an undergirth of tree roots that made me seasick as I navigated it.

She was kneeling in the grass beside a flowerbed built inside an eight-inch rock wall.

A new flowering bush sat next to her on the ground, and, as we headed in her direction, she half-turned to chuck another rock into the wheelbarrow waiting nearby.

"Mrs. Villa?"

When I called out, Lis's mom turned and waved. Her complexion was a little paler than usual and her eyes were underscored by purple. Tugging off her glove, she brushed the back of her hand across her glistening brow.

Hal eyed the collection of rocks in the barrow. "Would you like some help?"

She looked at him as if she was surprised by the offer. She probably was. Before her husband of thirty years had died, Lis's mom had been the sole gardener in the Villa home. Her husband worked long hours as an over-the-road driver and when he was home, had been content to spend his hours sprawled on the couch watching television.

She laughed softly. "No. But thank you. This is therapy for me."

Hal nodded. "I work with wood as therapy."

It was my turn to look surprised. I hadn't known that about him. But it explained the finishing work he'd been doing in his new cabin home.

"Would you two like some sun tea? I made some fresh this morning."

"I'd love some," Hal said at the same time I said, "We don't want to impose..."

Nancy snorted out a laugh. "Don't be silly, Joey. I'd like something cold right now myself. Besides, it gives me an excuse to sit for a spell."

Hal and I took seats at a round table in the shade of an old oak tree that arched over the patio, bathing it in soothing shade. Seeking solace for my unease, I stared out at Mary's well-kept yard as she went inside for the tea. My hands twisted nervously in my lap as I thought about the coming interview.

As if reading my frenzied thoughts, Hal looked over at me, his handsome face filled with understanding. He squeezed my hands. "Would you like me to lead this one?"

I nodded, feeling like a coward.

"I still can't believe it was hot enough to make tea this morning," Mary said as she exited the house carrying a pretty silver tray that was laden with tea things. "It sure looks like this summer's going to be a hot one."

"Thank you," I told her, taking one of the tall, frosty glasses. "This looks delicious." She'd put a thick slice of fresh lemon into the tea.

To my surprise, Hal ladled a couple of teaspoons of sugar into his, stirring it as Mary settled herself across from us. She smiled as I tasted my tea and groaned. "So good. I was thirstier than I realized."

"I'm glad you like it. Now, tell me why you're here. I know you're fond of me, and I'm certainly fond of you, but you look like you have something on your mind and, if I'm not mistaken, whatever it is it's got you upset."

I loved Mrs. Villa's characteristic directness. She'd always been like that. As a teen, it had sometimes made me unhappy. But I always knew where she stood on things, and there was comfort in that. The thought brought tears to my eyes. "I'm sorry..."

She tilted her head. "Is this about Viper Branch?"

I blinked in surprise. "How did you...?"

She laughed. "Joey, honey, how long have you lived in Deer Hollow?"

Despite my upset, I laughed with her. "The gossip mill is in full spin, I see."

"Of course. I knew you and Hal were asking questions about the murder almost the moment it happened." She favored Hal with a smile. "Everything your handsome PI does is of immediate interest to a certain subset of the local population."

"The women?" I guessed with a grin.

Hal shook his head and suddenly found his tea very interesting.

"We do have some questions for you," I said. "But they're just loose ends we need to tie up. It's not like we think you killed him...I mean..." I stammered to a halt, my face heating.

Nancy laughed. "Let me guess, you spoke to Ginnie Weldt and she told you that I visit Mary every week to sell her eggs?"

"Yes."

Nancy nodded. "It just so happens yesterday was my usual day to deliver to her."

"So you *were* there?" Hal asked.

Nancy shook her head. "Actually, no. I wasn't. I've been ill with the flu. I was pretty much unable to get out of bed until yesterday, but I still didn't have much energy. I stayed home and rested. If Betty hadn't brought me some soup and made me get up to eat, I probably would have stayed in bed until today."

I stared at my tea, dreading Hal's next question. He didn't hesitate.

"Mrs. Weldt told us you were there yesterday."

Nancy's pleasant expression faded, leaving behind a look of confusion. "She's wrong. I didn't go to Mary's this week."

"Is there anybody who can corroborate that?" Hal asked.

"Well, no. I'm sure you know I live here alone."

"Betty?" I asked hopefully.

Nancy shrugged. "She was here around four o'clock, but she didn't stay all that long. Maybe a half-hour."

"Did you maybe talk to one of your neighbors?" I asked, hoping she could point us toward someone who could take her off our list.

She shook her head. "Sorry."

"Do you have a computer, Mrs. Villa?"

Nancy blinked in surprise at Hal's question. "I... no. Just an e-reader. I love mysteries." She smiled, and I felt my chest go tight. She'd always loved mysteries. I could remember seeing her sitting on the couch reading when Lis and I stumbled home from a high school party at midnight, trying to act like we hadn't been drinking.

"Why do you ask?"

Hal sipped his tea before answering. "It might have told us you were here at a certain time."

"Oh. That makes sense." She shook her head. "Ginnie has really bad eyesight. She probably saw someone else's car and thought it was mine."

"What kind of car do you have?" Hal asked.

"A silver Chevy Malibu. It's not exactly distinctive."

Hal nodded.

"Look, I can promise you I wasn't there. Ginnie's mistaken me for someone else before, you know. To this day, she still thinks I ran over her dog."

Hal and I shared a look.

"She told you I hit her poor Thelma, didn't she?" Mary sighed. "I feel badly for her, I really do. But the truth is, everyone suspected Branch of letting that dog out of the house and nobody ever saw who hit her."

I frowned. "Then why is Ginnie blaming you?"

"Who knows. My guess is that Branch threatened her and she was scared. Since I was a regular visitor to the neighborhood and she wouldn't have to face me every day, I was the perfect person for her to blame."

My pulse picked up. "If it was Branch..."

Nancy nodded. "I hate to say it. Ginnie's not a terrible person or anything. She's just timid and a bit too nosy for her own good. But..." Nancy took a deep breath. "She has as good a motive as anyone to want Viper Branch dead."

The sound of shoes slapping against the sidewalk brought our attention toward the corner of the house.

"Hello? Mary? Are you out he..." A small woman with light brown hair that hung straight and thick to her shoulders slammed to a halt as she rounded the corner, her surprised gaze skimming over me and then Hal. She was dressed in a striped t-shirt dress and flipflops and held a small jar of something in one hand. She smiled. "I'm sorry. I didn't know you had company."

Mary stood up and motioned the woman over. "This is my cousin Betty. She and I have the egg business together."

Hal stood up and took Betty's diminutive hand in his, swamping it. "It's a pleasure to meet you, Betty."

Her eyelashes fluttered and she looked down, tugging her hand away. "The pleasure's all mine."

I stuck my hand out. "Hey, Betty. I'm Joey. Lis was telling me about the business you and Nancy have together. I think it's wonderful."

Betty's eyes lit up. "Thank you, Joey. You probably don't remember me, but I remember that you and Lis were always inseparable."

I had a vague recollection of meeting Lis's first cousin, once removed, aka "aunt" one of the times we'd played at the Weldt farm. My refreshed memory tugged another memory forward, of Lis explaining she called Betty her aunt just because it was easier. "I do remember you," I said, only half lying. "It's good to see you again."

"Can I get you some tea?" Nancy asked her cousin.

"No, thank you, dear. I'm on my way to the grocery. I just wanted to check-in and make sure you're okay."

"Feeling much better," Nancy told the other woman. "Your chicken noodle soup worked wonders."

Betty laughed. "It is magic." She extended her hand, offering Nancy the small jar filled with a viscous, dark gold liquid. "Take some of this. It has strong antiviral properties. But make sure you only take the amount I've written on the label."

Nancy nodded. "Thanks. Can you sit with us for a minute? We were just talking about Viper Branch's death."

The smile slid away from Betty's face, and her gray-blue gaze filled with tears. "That poor, poor man."

I was taken aback by her sympathies. "Branch was a friend of yours?" I asked, thinking I was being very diplomatic.

But something in my expression must have given my true feelings away. She sniffed, dragging her hand over her face to skim tears away. "I know he wasn't very popular, and I even understand why. Branch wasn't very nice to most...well...anybody really. But I understood him. I understood why he did what he did. He pushed people away so he wouldn't get hurt."

I doubted a sociopath would ever allow himself to get hurt by another person, but I didn't express my opinion. I was much more interested in hearing hers. "Has he been hurt in the past?"

Betty nodded eagerly. "Yes. But I'm not at liberty to tell that story."

"It's part of our investigation," Hal said. "If you know something that will help us, we need you to speak up."

She paled, her eyes going round. "It was the

pastor's wife. Angela Smythe hurt him deeply. He loved her and when she rebuffed him and left town he took it hard."

I was really struggling with the picture of Branch as victim, but I nodded politely. Maybe Betty really had seen another side to Viper Branch. "I'm sure that was upsetting."

She nodded. "He didn't have a chance, you know. Viper. His father was a monster. He mistreated everyone around him. I believe Viper was the way he was because he'd learned early on that love was painful."

"You liked him a lot, huh?" I asked gently.

Betty looked surprised. "Liked? No. Not at all. He was horrible to me. Mean and hateful. But I never let it bother me because I knew why he was that way. I guess you can say that he and I had something in common."

"You had an abusive parent too?" Hal asked.

Betty slid Nancy a look, and Mrs. Villa nodded, reaching out to clasp the other woman's hand. Betty sighed. "I did. Not nearly as bad as Eglund Branch, of course. But my daddy wasn't a nice man at all." She forced a smile. "I was very lucky to have the mama I had though. She was a strong positive influence. To this day I credit her with the fact that I grew up happy despite it all."

I was sipping coffee the next morning, thinking about our conversation with Nancy Villa and her cousin the night before when my cell phone rang. I answered it without looking at the ID. "Hello?"

"Joey?" Doc Beetle's gruff, almost angry voice was distinctive enough that I recognized it immediately.

Worry clenched a fist around my heart. "Is Spunky okay?"

"She's fine. Actually, she's doing very well."

"Oh, that's great news." I smiled with relief. Caphy trotted over and put her head on my knee, I scratched the wide space between her eyes and her tail whipped against the back of my chair.

"Yes. I'm calling to tell you she can come home this morning."

"So soon?"

"Yes. She's not fully recovered, of course, but she doesn't need to be here. She can rest and recover at home just as well. Can you pick her up at eleven?"

"Sure. I can do that."

"Good. I'll have her ready. And don't be late. I have an appointment to look at a pregnant cow at eleven fifteen."

I assured Doc I'd be there and hung up, giving Caphy an enthusiastic scrub behind the ears.

"Spunky's okay!" I told my happily bouncing pibl. "She's coming to stay with us today."

LaLee gave me one of her growly meows and jumped onto the table. I grimaced. Having a cat on the table and counters was not my favorite thing. But I was quickly learning that LaLee went where LaLee wanted to go, and my input on the matter was not appreciated.

The Siamese cat was training me well.

"You be on good behavior, Miss LaLee," I scolded her gently as she eyed me haughtily. "Spunky isn't feeling a hundred percent and she needs us to be kind."

Caphy suddenly shot to her feet. She barked once as the front door opened. I glanced at the clock, thinking it was a bit too early for Hal to be arriving, especially after having gone twenty-four hours the day before without sleep. Despite almost fourteen hours of catch-up sleep, it had taken a force of monumental will, better known as Caphy, to get me out of bed that morning. A pibl with a full bladder would not allow herself to be ignored.

"Joey?"

I blinked in surprise at the sound of Lis's voice. Setting my mug down on the table, I hurried to meet my friend at the front door.

Caphy got there first and was softening Lis up for the reconciliation when I stumbled to a nervous stop in front of her. "Hey."

Lis looked up from scratching my dog's ears and gave me a nervous smile. "Hey."

A throaty meow warned of LaLee's arrival. I bent to pick her up, not knowing how she'd react to Lis since they hadn't met before.

I needn't have bothered. The agile feline side-stepped my attempt to grab her and trotted over to Lis, winding herself around my friend's long, slender legs with a purr that threatened to rattle the glass in the windows.

"Oh, she's gorgeous!" Lis exclaimed, bending over to run a hand over LaLee's sleek gray-brown head.

Ever the jealous sibling, Caphy took the opportunity to stick her tongue up Lis's nose, prompting a startled exclamation and a giggle from my friend. "Thanks, Caph. Now I don't need to go to the doctor to have my nasal passages checked."

Caphy stood proudly back, tail whipping hard against the frame around the door, and barked once as if to say, "You're welcome."

"I'm really glad you came," I told Lis.

She straightened, frowning slightly. "I wanted to apologize. I totally over-reacted."

"No, you're right to be upset. I just want you to know I never for a minute suspected your mom. But we have to check out everybody who was around the area when it happened."

Lis nodded. "I know. I talked to mom last night, and she set me straight."

I held out my arms. "Friends?"

She laughed and accepted my hug, her eyes glossy with unshed tears. "Always."

When she pulled away, I asked, "Coffee?"

Lis nodded.

"I'll make a fresh pot. You want some fruit?"

"No, thanks. I had fruit and yogurt before I left mom's."

I grimaced. "This was only to hold me over until Hal gets here. He usually brings bagels or donuts when he comes."

She waggled her brows. "No wonder you're crazy about him."

"Right?" I agreed, laughing. "He's pretty special." I dumped the filter from the well of the coffee pot and dropped a new one in, scooping up coffee and hitting the button to start a new pot brewing.

"How's the whole living next door thing going?"

Lis was referring to the fact that Hal had recently bought and renovated a cabin on the adjoining property. It had actually been my Uncle Devon's cabin before he debunked Deer Hollow with my mom.

"Well, since there's about twenty acres of woods between us, I'm not sure I'd call it 'next door'." I shrugged. "But it's been great, actually. He's usually at the cabin four nights a week, and I see him every day when he's here. It's nice."

"He's still helping his brother with the practice in Indianapolis?"

I nodded. "He doesn't plan to quit Amity Investigations any time soon. But he *has* talked about opening an office here." I couldn't stop my grin and Lis grinned with me.

"Maybe he'll hire you to be his assistant."

I shook my head. "I'm holding out for partner."

She laughed. "I'm sure you'll get it. That man's smitten."

I wasn't sure if smitten was the right word, but coming from the most beautiful and glamorous woman I knew, it was really nice to hear. I poured Lis a cup of coffee and handed it over black, knowing she wouldn't waste calories on cream or sugar.

"How's your mom?" Lis's tone was gentle. I realized she wasn't sure how I was going to take the question. Truth was, I wasn't sure myself how I was going to take it until it was out there.

Then I took it pretty well. I thought. "Good, I think. I don't really know since I can't see her. But Devon's with her, keeping an eye out, so I'm assuming she's safe for the moment."

Lis looked surprised. "Your Uncle Devon's with her? Is there something romantic going on there?"

"It's not like that. He's just honoring a promise he made to my dad to keep an eye on us." Though

Devon Little wasn't my actual uncle, he'd been my dad's best friend since they were kids, and I'd always called him Uncle Devon because he was around as much or more than my own father had been. We'd actually been pretty close all my life. Until I discovered that he'd been lying to me about almost everything.

As *my* best friend since grade school, Lis had gotten pretty close to Devon too.

"Hopefully they'll catch Medford soon, and she can get back to having a real life."

Garland Medford was a criminal with ties to drugs, sex trafficking, and murder. Medford's organization was wide and well-connected, including law enforcement and a couple levels of government. My parents had gotten involved with someone close to Medford, someone who'd stolen something from him that he'd treasured, and they'd inadvertently put themselves into the crosshairs of the villain. When my parents' plane had been taken down by one of Medford's agents, killing my father and the other passenger, whom I'd believed at the time was my mother, Devon and my mom had been forced into hiding to keep her from suffering the same fate.

I sighed. "Hopefully." I forced a smile I didn't feel. "Are you going to be around tonight? I was thinking of stopping by Junior's to get the makings of a barbeque."

She blew across the surface of her hot coffee. "That would be fun."

"I was going to try to get Arno to come. You don't mind, do you?"

She took a sip and grimaced. I wasn't sure if the grimace was because the coffee was too hot or because I wanted to have Arno over for dinner. "Not at all," she finally said, setting the mug down to look at me. "He's probably pretty messed up about his mom right now."

I nodded. "He is. And Hal and I haven't had a chance to tell him what we've learned so far. I thought we could do that and then maybe take his mind off his troubles for a while with some fishing."

Lis's eyes went wide. "Fishing!" She clapped her hands. "I haven't gone fishing for ages."

"Probably not since we were ten," I agreed. When my dad had taken us out in the rickety wooden boat we'd owned. He and Devon had eventually sunk the boat. Or rather the boat had sunk *them*. And we'd become land-locked fishermen after that.

Lis stared at her mug for a minute. I glanced at the clock on the wall. Hal was late. I considered giving him a call but realized that would be too stalkerish. When Lis hadn't spoken for a full two minutes, I reached out and touched her hand. "Is something wrong?"

She jerked a bit as if I'd yanked her from her

thoughts. Then she smiled. "No. I was just remembering your high school graduation party down by
that pond."

I realized where her thoughts had gone and
grinned. It had been a great party. A beautiful day,
hot and sunny. My parents had surprised me with a
floating island that day, and it had been so much fun
diving off of the wooden platform into the water.

The pond had been new then, cleaner and sans
weeds and muck. The water had sparkled silver and
blue in the sun. And I'd been surrounded by all my
friends. Someone...Billy Petrisk, I thought–who was
actually a year younger than we were but whose
family had been friends with my family for as long
as I could remember–had snuck a jar of Devon's
homemade moonshine into the party and spiked
everyone's lemonade with it.

Music blared across our property, shouts and
laughter rising regularly above it as the party turned
slightly tipsy. And at one point I couldn't find Lis. Or
Arno.

"I'm a little surprised you two never got together
after that. He was obviously crazy about you."

She shrugged. "I left for college and he...didn't."

Arno had taken a job in town to keep an eye on
his mom. Other than a few months at the law
enforcement training academy, he'd never left. I'd
often thought resentment over opportunities lost
was at the core of Arno's innate crankiness. Though

he'd never said a word about being stuck in Deer Hollow.

"I'm glad you're going to be here. Arno can use all the support we can give him right now."

She nodded, still looking thoughtful.

"What else?"

"I was just thinking. Mom told me about her arrangement with Aunt Betty."

"The eggs." I nodded.

"It got me to thinking. You might want to talk to Betty about Viper Branch."

I felt my eyes go wide. "You think she might have killed him?"

Lis laughed, shaking her head. "No. Just the opposite. She actually seemed to like the man. I think she's the only person I've ever spoken to who didn't hate him. I just thought she might be able to give you a different...perspective...on his life and him."

"We actually spoke to her briefly at your mom's house yesterday, but I wouldn't mind asking her a few more questions. It might be good to get her on her own to talk about him. Does she still live at her family's farm west of the Hollow?"

"She does. If you want, I can take you out there."

"I might take you up on that." A car door slammed outside, and I glanced at the clock again. It had to be Hal. He was twenty minutes late, but I figured he'd probably slept in. He'd earned the extra sleep. "Hal's here." I jumped up and hurried toward the front door, trailing Caphy and Lis in my wake.

My friend was chuckling as I reached for the door handle. I glowered at her. "What's so funny?"

"I can't figure out if you're more excited to see Hal or the baked goods he's bringing you."

"Har de har," I told her, my lips twitching. But she wasn't alone. I wasn't sure which I was more excited about either.

When I opened the door, it didn't take long for me to decide. Hal leaned down and pressed his lips against mine. Warmth infused my entire body from that kiss, and I almost forgot about the wonderful-smelling paper bag in Hal's hand until Lis cleared her throat behind me.

We jumped apart and Lis laughed. "Sorry to disturb, but I was wondering if anyone noticed Caphy was licking the grease spot on that bag?"

Hal and I looked down to find my naughty Pibl caught mid-lick, and Hal jerked it up and away.

I couldn't help wondering how many times that had happened. Caphy seemed very comfortable with the action.

Hal lifted the bag, grinning at Lis. "I brought enough for three."

I narrowed my gaze at him. "How did you know...?"

He shook his head. "I didn't. But I brought two chocolate-covered cream-filled donuts for you, and

I'm sure you'll be thrilled to share one with your best friend."

I frowned thoughtfully. I did love Lis. But maybe giving her one of my donuts was over and above what should be expected of friends.

Lis gave Hal a brief hug, chuckling. "I'm surprised you don't know her better than that by now," she told Hal. To me she said, "I'm taking mom shopping and then out to lunch, so I'd better get going. What time do you want me here tonight?"

"How about seven o'clock?"

"Perfect. I'll bring wine."

I closed the door behind Lis and leaned against it, smiling.

"I'm glad to see she got over being mad at us."

It was kind of him to include himself in that since I was pretty sure Lis had only really been mad at me. "She talked to her mom and Nancy encouraged her to let it go."

"That's one classy woman," Hal said, dropping an arm around my shoulders and drawing me close so he could kiss the top of my head. "Deer Hollow has a few classy women. Classy and beautiful."

I flushed with pleasure. "I know you were talking about Lis, but I'm going to pretend you meant me too."

He shoved the bag at me. "I was talking about you and you know it. Stop fishing for compliments."

I peeked inside, surprised to see three donuts in the bag. "Which one is yours," I asked.

"The one without dog spit on it," he responded as we headed to the kitchen. "What was that about tonight?" He poured coffee for himself and held the pot up, a question in his green gaze. I grabbed my mug and let him fill it. I couldn't have a donut without coffee to dunk it in.

"I thought we could pick up some steaks at Juniors while we're out and about. I invited Lis to come over, and I'm hoping to entice Arno to come."

The look on Hal's face told me he didn't believe that was going to happen.

"You don't think he'll come?"

"I don't think he's left the station since he brought his mother in. He's even showering and sleeping there."

I shook my head. "I'm sure Mary wouldn't want him to isolate himself from everybody."

"No. But you know Arno, he thinks he knows better than anybody else." It wasn't said with any accusation in Hal's voice. It was simply the truth.

One I couldn't disagree with. "Well, I've got the big guns."

"Lis?"

"Yeah. They had a thing in high school. I've always thought they'd make an adorable couple."

He shook his head. "Arno hasn't ever shown any signs that he's interested."

"That's because you don't know what to look for. The more Arno ignores her, the more I know he's crazy about her."

Hal didn't look convinced. "If you say so." He sat down at the table with his coffee. "Did Lis share anything useful this morning?"

"Only that she thought we should talk to her Aunt Betty about Branch since she's probably the only one in Deer Hollow who liked him."

Hal swallowed a bite of donut. "So, this relationship she had with Branch, you think it was some kind of prison bride thing?"

I laughed. "Maybe. I guess she might just like bad boys."

"Try sociopathic boys," Hal said, taking another bite of his donut. "And speaking of sociopaths..." he said with a grin.

"Ugh!" I responded. "I'm guessing that's your way of telling me George Shulz is first on the interview docket this morning?"

"Got it in one."

8

The tiny yellow clapboard house on a dead-end street in Deer Hollow served as both George Shulz's office and his home.

A large, gold and black sign in the yard with George Shulz's name and letters spelled out in six-inch-high script verified that we'd come to the right place. Though my previous experience there would have made it difficult to forget the place or its owner.

Despite the neatly trimmed yard and freshly painted house, the place gave off a slightly shabby air that I suspected was strictly in my mind.

We followed the winding brick sidewalk to a front door that was painted a dark green. As he'd done before, Hal stopped with his hand on the knob and looked at me. "Are you ready?"

"Is one ever ready for George Shulz?" I responded.

He shook his head, and that was all the response needed. Hal shoved the door open and we were greeted by a meth lab stench and a chorus of meows and hisses. Hal indicated I should precede him into the house, and I gave him a look.

As if realizing his mistake, he gave me a crooked smile and took point, stepping in ahead of me.

I couldn't shake the feeling that one of us should have gone in high and one low.

Then I realized that since he was over six feet tall and I...wasn't...nature had already taken care of that for us.

Hal stopped just inside the door as a particularly heartfelt hiss, followed by a dog-sized growl, punctuated a breach in the feline disharmony.

I peered around him and made a small sound of alarm.

Either George had found a rare breed of dog that looked just like a striped cat, or he'd rescued a cat who'd undergone experiments with human growth hormone.

"That's the biggest cat I've ever seen," Hal murmured. He sneezed several times, pulling a hankie from the pocket of his jeans.

"You took your antihistamines?" I asked, my hand on his arm.

He nodded and blew his nose, gaze locked warily on the creature draped over Shulz's messy desk.

The cat had to weigh thirty pounds and looked

to be over twenty inches long. "Also the angriest," I agreed. If I didn't know better, I'd think someone had thrown a handful of magic dust over George Shulz and turned him into a monster-sized cat.

"Hal Amity," said an oily voice from shadows inside the room. "Vehicular manslaughter. A continuing danger to society but at least you paid your bill when I sent it to you."

Hal shifted slightly as I shoved past him to watch the show. "Right name, wrong business connection," he told the shadow.

Stepping into the light, Shulz cocked his greasy, dark-brown head and narrowed his gaze. "Hal Amity. Killer of children..."

"Stop right there," Hal said, angrily. "You know that's not true."

The lawyer's dark gaze sparkled with humor. He was a veritable Bad Santa just having a little fun at someone else's expense. Shulz shook his head. "I don't care how I know you. You're not an active case, so I'm done with you. Go away."

Hal seemed a bit taken aback by the early cessation of the usual game. He eyed Shulz carefully, and I couldn't help wondering if he was checking to see if the man was ill.

For my part, I don't see how he could *not* be ill given the circumstances he lived and worked in.

Apparently deeming itself the initiator of expelling action, a.k.a. a feline bouncer, the massive orange and black striped cat jumped down from Shulz's desk, the floor quivering under its weight, and gave us another heartfelt growl.

"We're not leaving just yet, Shulz," Hal said. "I'm going to have to ask you to call off your watch-cat."

Shulz's thin lips turned upward at the corners. "I don't think so. State your business and leave."

I still found it hard to believe Hal had actually worked with Shulz once upon a time. When Shulz's hate-filled dark eyes found me, widening slightly with interest, I nearly turned and fled the building. But my pride wouldn't let me run like a scared little girl. I lifted my chin and held his arrogant gaze.

He looked down his short, round nose at me, the thin lips curving into a mean smile. "Joey Fulle, unintelligent bumpkin with no common sense. Fortunately, I've never had the misfortune of having you as a client. Though there have certainly been enough legal opportunities in your family to keep me in Spam and noodles for decades."

I forced myself not to respond. My unwavering gaze hopefully sent the message that his words didn't affect me. First of all, who even ate Spam anymore?

Apparently seeing my silence as encouragement to go on, Shulz tipped his head in thought and I braced for another salvo. It came in a different form than I'd expected. "Did you find out yet? I warned you she didn't want to be with you. Has Joline shown her true colors yet?"

Despite my best efforts, I flinched.

His smile widened. "Ah. I see you've learned that I don't lie."

"Leave her alone, Shulz," Hal growled out.

"Or what, boy?" the ugly little man said. "You'll wallop me? I'm sure Deputy Willager wouldn't be happy to have you in his jail, seeing as you're supposed to be finding a way to save mommy dearest from murder charges."

"Mary didn't kill that man," I said before I even knew my lips were moving. I surprised myself. Until that moment, I hadn't realized how thoroughly I believed Mary Willlager was innocent. "She didn't kill your best friend, Viper Branch."

He laughed easily, showing gray, uneven teeth that looked as if they'd never been brushed. "I don't have friends, Joey Fulle. But he *was* a client. I'll confirm that."

"What were you defending him from?" Hal asked as the cat swiped a plum-sized paw in our direction, claws unsheathed as it hissed.

"Attorney-Client Privilege," Shulz said, staring fondly at the massive cat.

The cat leaped forward suddenly, swiping its claws over Hal's shoe. He pulled the foot back, his jaw tightening. "Call it off, or I'm going to subdue the thing my way, Shulz."

The lawyer shrugged, his expression cold. He'd like us to believe he didn't care what happened to the cat, but I could see just the slightest tension around his eyes. The man wasn't the sociopath he pretended to be. He cared about his stinky cats.

He was just a horse's behind.

"Come, Goliath. Here kitty."

The cat turned its oversized head and looked at Shulz, its striped tail whisking a tumbleweed of cat hair out from under the desk as it considered whether it would obey.

Shulz pulled a small plastic bowl off the counter by the coffee maker and the cat whipped around, prancing heavily toward the lawyer, its massive belly swaying from side to side with the movement.

Shulz placed the bowl on the floor and ran his hand over the cat's wide back before straightening back up.

Even standing where I was, I could see the filth caked in Shulz's ragged fingernails.

"Now tell us what kind of business you were doing with Branch?" Hal persisted. "We have an eye-witness account that said you paid the man regular visits at his home."

Shulz crossed his filthy hands in front of him and stared at us.

"I'm surprised you'd be friends with a man who regularly hurt cats," I ventured, just to see if he'd react.

He didn't.

"I'll find out one way or the other, Shulz. I'm assuming you'd rather not pay a visit to the Sheriff's station as a person of interest?"

"You can't arrest me. You're not a cop."

"Actually, I've been deputized by Deputy Willager. I can lock you up and forget you're there for several hours. In fact, I'm hoping you give me just one good reason to do it."

Shulz stared at us a moment longer, but some of the belligerence had left his expression. Unfortunately, it had been replaced by rage. "Mr. Branch was filing to become an LLC."

Hal blinked in surprise. "He what?"

Shulz inclined his head. "Branch was starting a publishing company."

"Publishing what, exactly?"

Shulz looked suddenly smug. "The business was going to be called The Proud Sociopath."

Hal's gaze narrowed. "You haven't answered my question. What was he going to publish?"

Shulz shrugged. "This and that. He had a blog and was monetizing it."

I fought a hysterical laugh. "Viper Branch was monetizing being a Sociopath?"

Barking out a delighted laugh, Shulz nodded. "His blog was actually quite popular, with thousands of subscribers. He also had a hundred thousand subscribers on his video channel."

I didn't want to believe that a hundred thousand people would be entertained by a sociopath's rantings, but I'd seen enough depravity on the news that I reluctantly accepted it as a possibility. "Surely he couldn't make a living that way?"

Shulz just continued to smile.

Hal narrowed his gaze. "If I dig into this little venture of Branch's, am I going to find your disgusting fingerprints on it?"

Shulz shrugged. "You might call me a paid consultant."

Clearly repulsed, Hal shook his head. "Do you have any idea who might have wanted Branch dead?" He ground the question out through his teeth as if he had to force himself to ask it.

"The man was a sociopath, Amity. People he met could be divided almost perfectly into two camps. The camp who wanted him to cease existing, and the camp who couldn't adore him hard enough. I'll let you do the math on that."

Hal was quiet as he pulled his Escalade away from Shulz's office. I couldn't believe what we'd just learned. It was all so surreal. Tucked away in my bucolic little world at Deer Hollow, I tried to keep the ugliness of the world at bay. Though it occasionally made itself impossible to ignore, such as when a dead body dropped in my path, I mostly managed to live in blissful ignorance, with the idea that the debauchery lived far away from my world.

But I was having to come to grips with learning that a dark menace thrived mere blocks from the places I frequented...an ugly blotch of inhumanity and evil...and it took the wind right out of my sails.

I shivered at the thought, pulling Hal's brooding attention over to me. "I'm afraid we're going to have to search Branch's place," he said.

I grimaced, trying to remember if I was up-to-date on my tetanus shots. "Didn't Arno's people already go through his house and Mary's?"

"Yes. But with this new information, I think we need to take another look. The deputies wouldn't have known what they were looking for."

I nodded, knowing he was right. "Okay, but we might want to get our shots first."

Hal grinned. "I don't think there's a shot to protect against evil."

He was right, of course. But, sighing, I couldn't help thinking that, whoever had killed Branch had found the only real cure.

*a*s we walked through the door into Branch's double-wide trailer, I found myself doing a full-body clench. My mind conjured up the possibility that the dead man's malevolence might have filled the air and coated the flat surfaces like dust, wafting up with our every movement to infuse my sinuses and rot my brain.

I expected a foul stench at the very least, sulfur-based, as if the home covered a portal to Hell, its gases leaking from the cracks to permeate the small space.

What I found instead was a tidy home with worn but well-kept furnishings and even a few plants sitting on the windowsill of the small kitchen to brighten up the space.

Yes, they were cacti, prickly and repellent, but

their vibrant green arms lifted hopefully toward the sun and made me think of life and living.

"Not what I was expecting," I murmured to Hal.

He nodded, his gaze sliding to the laptop computer on the square kitchen table. The table and chairs were painted a cheerful yellow. Another incongruity in the land of evil things. "I'll see what I can find in his computer. Will you search the drawers?" Hal nodded toward a short counter next to the refrigerator. It appeared to be a makeshift desk area, with two cabinets consisting only of drawers and a small chair tucked into a gap between them.

I walked over and tugged out the chair, stepping in front of it to yank open the wide, shallow center drawer. Bright, happy yellow or no, I couldn't sit down in the chair. In fact, I wished I had a pair of latex gloves like CSU people wore so my skin wouldn't have to touch the drawers.

Like the rest of the house, the big drawer was tidy, almost to the point of OCD. Pens were collected neatly in one cheap plastic basket, rubber bands in another, paper clips in yet another basket. In the center was a neatly stacked pile of paper. I pulled those out and laid them on the counter. The papers on top were clipped together and, flipping quickly through them, I saw that they were bills. Judging by the date neatly written across the top sheet in black ink, the bills had all been paid.

The next group consisted of unpaid bills if the

lack of a date on the top was any indication. I flipped quickly through them, seeing one from Shulz Law Offices for a thousand dollars. There was a large stamp at the top in red proclaiming the bill as past due. Apparently filing for an LLC was an expensive proposition. I wondered if George Shulz would have killed Branch for not paying his bill.

Maybe those hadn't been knife wounds in the victim after all. Maybe they'd been teeth and claw marks from a freakishly large striped cat.

"This is interesting," Hal said, tearing me from my fantasyland musings.

I turned around. "What?"

"His search history is filled with botanical information."

"Botanical? As in, which plants might be used to poison a sweet, elderly retriever?" I scrunched up my face with disgust.

"This seems almost too easy." Hal shook his head.

I turned back to my task, my mind racing with the possible outcome if we could prove Branch actually *had* poisoned Spunky. It wouldn't be good for Mary.

I set the bills aside and blinked down at the last pile. They were letters. I quickly read through the one on top, grimacing. It was a love letter.

"Ew."

Hal glanced up. "What?"

"Love letters. How is this even possible?"

"I'll never understand some women's obsession with bad men." He shook his head.

Of course, my PI wouldn't understand that. He was too good of a man. His mind just didn't work that way.

I skimmed through the letter on top and then three more like it. Each letter was signed by a different woman. It was as if he'd saved a sample from each. I had a thought. "Did you find his website?"

Hal frowned, his fingers dancing over the keys. "Here it is. I went with the name of his LLC. It's the same as his blog."

I walked over and stood, looking over his shoulder. "Is there anything about women?"

"What do you mean?"

"I don't know. Mean or condescending posts? Sociopathic Dating tips?"

We shared a grin.

Hal turned back to the screen. "Let's see... On the front page is a ranting post about people who drive slow in the left lane." He shook his head. "Who knew Branch and I would ever agree on something."

"Except he's recommending euthanasia for those people. I'm assuming you wouldn't go that far."

Hal seemed to be considering it.

I laughed and slapped his shoulder. "What else?"

He scrolled down a few posts, reciting the

themes. "Ways to scam online stores to get stuff for free. How to fool people into thinking you have emotions." He shook his head. "There's nothing here about women."

"How about in the older posts?"

Hal found the list of older posts and read them off. "Why Religion Sucks, Don't be Fooled by the Animal Protection Idiots, Emasculating Men who Don't act like Men..." Hal looked up. "Branch didn't discriminate here. He basically hated everybody."

I nodded, scanning the rest of the list. One title caught my attention, and I pointed to it. "There, Heartless in the Hollow. Let's see what that's about."

What it was about was how to make women fall in love with you without letting on that you felt nothing for them.

"Study the science of visual clues," the article said. "Learn how to indicate love and affection so they'll feel comfortable giving you what you want..."

I grimaced. "Cold. That would be enough to make any woman want to kill him." I had a horrible thought. "You don't think Mary and Branch..."

Hal shrugged. "In this business, I've learned that anything's possible. We'll need to talk to Mary again."

I nodded.

A window in the living room shattered and light flared, flickering over the walls as smoke quickly filled the air.

Hal jerked to his feet. "Fire!" He grabbed my arm and dragged me toward the exterior door on the sidewall of the kitchen. He turned the knob and shoved.

It didn't move.

He threw his body at it again, and it rattled in the frame but held.

Hal glanced nervously toward the fire spreading quickly through the front room.

I coughed as the kitchen filled with the choking smoke. "Now what?"

"I'm thinking." Hal started coughing too, deep, chest ripping coughs that brought him to his knees. He pulled me down with him. "Stay low."

Hal and I looked at the door. He jerked his gaze to me. "Did you see a key in that drawer?"

"No." But I crawled quickly back there, yanking the drawer open and rifling through it. In frustration, I ripped the drawer out and dumped its contents onto the floor so I could see better. Hal made quick work of the other drawers but didn't have any better luck than I'd had.

By that point, we were coughing so hard I thought I'd cough up a lung.

Hal eyed the flames licking around the door from the living room. Then we both skimmed a look toward the small window over the sink. I was pretty sure I wouldn't be able to fit my butt through the small space, let alone Hal's large bulk.

"We need to go out through the living room," he said, his expression grim.

A thunderous roar filled the other room, and a blast of super-heated air blew us backward. I slammed into the wall on the far side, the impact driving all the air out of my lungs. I was only dimly aware of Hal crashing to the floor beside me as stars burst before my gaze and I started to blackout.

I fought disorientation as the world seemed to spin around me, my eyes and lungs stinging violently under a never-ending assault from the caustic smoke. I became vaguely aware of hands gripping my arms, and then I was flying. I think I let off a little scream as my body left the floor and something hard cut into my belly. I heard a crash and voices and then felt myself being shoved.

My eyes came open as I started to fall. My arms came up. I screamed as I dropped. But then I landed, and it was okay. There was no pain.

"Joey?" An urgent voice said. "Open your eyes, Joey." I knew the voice, but I couldn't put together why it was there. Hands gently slapped my face, and my eyes snapped open. I regretted it immediately as violent coughing overtook me.

"How is she?" More coughing, only it wasn't coming from me. I looked up into Hal's worried face. It was black with soot and blood ran from several cuts on his face.

I reached out a hand. "You got us out."

He clasped my hand and raised it to his lips, kissing it as his eyes found mine. "Only because we got really lucky. Arno was here."

My brain finally registered the other voice, and I turned to find him. But he was gone. He was several yards away, pacing the yard and yelling into his cell phone. I gradually became aware of sirens screaming toward us. "Why...?"

Hal shook his head. "I don't know."

I smiled, my hand finding his sooty cheek and caressing it. "You don't know what I was going to ask."

"Whatever it is, I don't know." He grabbed me under the arms. "Sit up. The ambulance is here. You need..." He couldn't finish as another round of violent coughing took him. In apparent sympathy for his coughing, my lungs tried to escape my chest through my esophagus too.

Arno returned. "Let's get you guys some oxygen. Can you walk?"

I nodded, and they helped me to my feet. I weeble-wobbled for a moment and then Hal and I made our way toward the ambulance that had just arrived. The EMTs were pulling out a stretcher as we approached. Hal shook his head. "You won't need that."

We all but collapsed onto the back of the ambulance, and a tech clapped an oxygen mask over my nose and mouth.

I tried to push it toward Hal as he succumbed to another round of coughing, but he shook his head. "You first."

Pushing at his hand, I took several good breaths and handed it to him. "We'll share."

He gave me a smile before covering his face with it.

Arno came striding up, his face dark with anger. "Can you tell me what happened?" he demanded of Hal.

Hal shook his head. "Not specifically. We were in the kitchen looking at Branch's computer and heard a crash, then the fire. I'm guessing it was a Molotov-cocktail-type device. A second one came through the window a few minutes later. It must have been a big one. It exploded pretty good in the flames."

Arno nodded. He watched the fire truck barrel up the street. "I smelled gasoline. You're lucky I came to my mom's for some stuff."

"You didn't see him?" I asked Arno.

He frowned. "I wish I had. I was in the house looking for her meds. When I came back out, I saw the flames and ran over here. I was calling it into Fire and Rescue when an iron pot came sailing through the window." He rubbed one arm. "It felt like it had been shot from a ball launcher."

Hal chuckled. "Sorry about that. Adrenaline."

"I can certainly understand that."

"Did you find what you needed at your mom's house?" Hal asked, watching Arno carefully.

Arno's return glare told me there was some kind of message passing between them that I'd missed.

"I did a thorough search of the place and found nothing that would suggest she'd been drugged. I took the eggs and anything else that might have been doctored. I'll have the lab test it all, looking for drugs."

Hal nodded.

Arno pointed a finger at him. "But that doesn't mean I'm buying your theory that she killed Branch under the influence of some drug." He skimmed his glare to include me. "Excuse me." Arno walked away to instruct the fire personnel. They didn't look happy with his instruction. "The trailer's a lost cause," Arno told them as they unwound their hoses. "Focus on the garage and the nearest homes."

The firemen looked at him and shook their heads.

"Arno's not winning any friends telling them how to do their jobs," I murmured to Hal.

He shook his head. "He just can't help himself."

I nodded, my gaze sliding to Mary's cute bungalow wavering behind a wall of heat and ash. It would be a shame if her house caught fire too.

Seeing the house and the growing fleet of emergency vehicles clogging the street, and Mary's driveway brought me back to the night of the murder. And a memory clicked into place. I looked at Hal. "Spunky!"

He frowned. "The dog? What about her?"

"I'm supposed to pick her up at eleven this morning. What time is it?"

"Ten thirty. I'm sure Doc will keep her for a while."

Shaking my head, I shoved to my feet, dropping the mask to the floor of the ambulance. "He told me not to be late."

Hal reached a hand toward my arm. "Joey, you need to sit here for a bit and let your body recover..."

"I promised Mary I'd take care of her dog. I'm not going to drop the ball the first time I'm asked to honor that promise." I knew I was being overly emotional, irrational, but I felt too strongly about the issue to listen to reason. I started marching toward Hal's car. "Hopefully, we can get out. There's about a thousand cars and trucks here right now."

I was exaggerating, but not by much. Deer Hollow didn't have many fires, and it seemed that everybody wanted in on the action.

Hal said something to Arno as I hurried toward his car. I couldn't hear Arno's response, but I could guess what it was. He'd want us to give him a statement.

He'd get his statement, as much good as it would do him. I hadn't seen or heard anything before the front window exploded and spit fire at us.

But before that statement was going to happen. I had an injured, elderly dog who needed me to do what I'd promised. And I had every intention of doing it.

Even if I had to walk all the way to the vet's office.

10

*F*ortunately, Hal didn't make me walk. We arrived at Doc Beetle's office five minutes ahead of my eleven o'clock deadline. Doc's assistant, Sally, glanced up as we came through the door. I hadn't expected to see her there.

Sally smiled at me and slid a surprised gaze over Hal. "My goodness, did you two fall into a campfire?"

I brushed at my sooty shorts and tee, feeling self-conscious. I figured by the way Sally's pert nose wrinkled that we smelled like a campfire too. "Someone threw a Molotov cocktail into Viper Branch's trailer while we were in there searching it."

"Oh, no! Are you okay?" Her expression turned instantly concerned.

"We're okay," Hal said in a voice that sounded scratchy and rough. "But the trailer's gone."

Sally shook her head. "What is going on in our

little town?" The petite, middle-aged woman was pretty and spry, but she had circles under her hazel eyes that hadn't been there the last time I'd seen her. "How's your mom," I asked.

Sally shook her head, her eyes shiny with unshed tears. "Not good. I brought her back to Deer Hollow with me so I can spend more time with her."

I didn't ask what her mother was suffering from, feeling as if it was none of my business. If Sally wanted us to know, she'd tell us.

"I'm so sorry, Sally. But I'll bet Doc's glad to have you back," I said, offering her a gentle smile.

She gave a watery laugh, nodding. "It's a good thing I came back when I did. The man's a great vet and a wonderful human being, but his office management skills leave something to be desired." She shook her head. "Guess where I found the lab reports for Spunky Willager?"

I opened my mouth to respond but Hal beat me to it. "In the refrigerator."

Sally gave him an astonished glance and then lifted her brows at me. "Apparently, it makes sense in the male brain."

I laughed with her. "Is Spunky ready to go?"

Sally nodded. "She's weak and she'll need to be on special food for a few weeks. Her stomach was irritated by the poison, I'm afraid." Sally glowered down at the instructions she had in front of her. "Antibiotics and antacids. It's all written up here."

She handed the sheet of paper and a bill to Joey. "Doc said to give this bill to Mary when you have the chance. There's no hurry."

I nodded. Eyeing the unhappy expression on Sally's face, I tried to think of a way to get her to open up about what she was thinking. She'd been away for several weeks tending to her mother, but Sally was well-connected in the gossip circles and, though she rarely spilled what she knew, I figured Doc's assistant might have information that would help. Folding the papers in half, I slipped them into my purse. "It's terrible, what happened to Spunky."

Sally expelled air as if she'd been holding her breath. "It's just evil. That man..." She shook her head. "I'm sorry. I just feel so strongly about people abusing animals. I think that type of person should go to jail." Her hand shook as she rubbed her brow.

"I know how you feel. I don't understand people who'd do that to a helpless animal," I agreed.

She dropped into her chair behind the desk. "I know I shouldn't talk about this..." Sally glanced at Hal.

"It's okay. Hal and I are helping Arno with the investigation."

Her eyes widened in surprise. "You're probably wondering if I can help."

I nodded.

"I can tell you that Viper Branch had a rough start in life. His father was cruel to everyone and everything. I'm afraid he didn't have a very good role model."

"But?" Hal asked, no doubt sensing as I did that Sally had more to add to her statement.

"But, in his case, I believe it's more a nature than nurture thing. I'm pretty sure Branch Senior was a sociopath, and I believe he passed that trait on to his son."

"A true sociopath?" I asked.

"Yes. My friend works at Social Services for the county. She remembers all the times Viper was taken away from his father. She spent time with him. Spoke with him on numerous occasions, trying to find out if he was in danger in that home. What she determined was that Viper didn't really care where he ended up. He seemed to have no feelings for his father, bad or good. He showed no emotion. No remorse. No care of any kind for anyone around him."

"What about his mother?" I couldn't help asking.

Sally shrugged. "She was never in the picture as far as I know. I think there might have been mental competency issues."

"Do you remember anyone Branch might have harmed growing up who could still hold a grudge?" Hal asked

She slid her gaze to Hal, chewing her bottom lip. "It's not really my place to say."

So, there *was* someone. "It's important, Sally," I

told her. "The fire at Branch's home today proves that we're still not safe. There's a killer out there, and whoever it is, they're trying to stop us from finding out his or her identity. We won't be safe until we catch that person."

She chewed her lip again, finally nodding. "My friend told me a story about a young high school girl who barged into the offices one day when Branch was there, screaming about it being his fault that her daddy was dead."

I felt my eyes widen with shock. "Why? What happened?" Hope soared. Maybe we'd found the lead that would take us to the killer.

Sally shook her head. "I don't remember the details. And my friend has since moved to Florida, and I've lost track of her."

I deflated, my hopes dashed.

"But maybe you could talk to the girl, well woman now, who made the charge. I believe she recently moved back to Deer Hollow."

"What's her name?" Hal asked, pulling out his cell phone, no doubt to jot down the information so he could get her address after we left.

"Her name is Samantha Powers. I believe she recently moved into the new Hollows subdivision."

My pulse spiked at the familiar name, but I did my best to hide it. A quick glance at Hal told me he'd recognized the name too.

Samantha Powers was one of the ladies who'd been on the flower committee with Mary.

Spunky lay quietly on the back seat, her head resting on her front legs and her eyes shifting back and forth between Hal and me as we talked on the way to my house. I'd been a little conflicted about taking on the sick dog before picking her up. I was worried I'd mess something up and Spunky would take a turn for the worse. I didn't want to have to be the one to tell Mary I made her dog sicker.

But all of my doubts had fled the moment Sally lead the big retriever out to us in the waiting room. Spunky settled her warm, brown gaze on me, her thick fringe of a tail whipping the air happily behind her as if we'd been friends forever.

"Such a good girl, Miss Spunky." I reached into the back seat, and she lifted her head, swiping her tongue over my palm as I spoke to her.

Hal studied her in the rear-view mirror. "That is possibly the sweetest dog I've ever met."

When I swung my gaze to him, he quickly clarified. "Caphy excluded, of course."

I chuckled. "Don't worry. I'm not going to hold it against you. Caphy's awesome, but she's too high energy to be considered sweet. Friendly, energetic, and wonderful, yes. But sweet implies a gentleness my pibl will probably never have."

Hal nodded. He pulled into my driveway and drove toward the house. As he turned off the engine, I could already hear Caphy barking a frantic greeting. I looked at the drool-painted window in my living room and grinned as her adorable head appeared there, her ears flopping jauntily as she bounced up and put her paws onto the sill.

An elegant, cream and brown-gray form leaped up next to Caphy's head. LaLee peered out at us through curious dark blue eyes.

"The gang's all there," I said to Hal.

He opened the back door and clipped the leash onto Spunky's collar. "I'll walk her around to see if she needs to do any business," he told me.

I nodded. "I think I'll put a leash on Caphy so she doesn't run Spunky over trying to be best friends."

"Good idea," Hal agreed.

Despite my concerns for her behavior, Caphy gave Spunky a gentle sniff-over and then fell into step beside her new friend as Spunky explored the front yard. The two dogs walked around and took turns peeing on every tree and bush near the house. Then Spunky dropped, panting, to her belly in the shade, clearly too tired to explore any further.

Hal left to shower the smoke and soot off and change his clothes. I planned to do the same. We agreed to meet back at my house in a half-hour and, after going to speak to Samantha Powers, Hal promised to take me to lunch.

I settled Spunky in one of Caphy's big foam beds in my bedroom with water and a fan in case she got too hot from the afternoon sun shining through the windows.

I went to close my bedroom door so the other animals couldn't pester her, but a sleek beige and brown blur shot through before I could. LaLee screeched to a halt when she saw Spunky and then slowly approached the big dog.

Spunky gave her tail a single wag as she watched the cranky feline approach but she didn't lift her head off the bed.

To my shock, LaLee didn't hiss or spit at the intruder in her space. Instead, she stopped in front of the retriever and offered her own form of what sounded like a very civilized greeting. Then she touched noses with Spunky and turned away, jumping up onto my bed and lying down, her gaze on our weak and weary guest.

"You want to keep her company?" I asked the cat as I ran a hand along her sleek back and sides.

"Meow," she responded in her throaty voice.

"Okay, you be nice now." I headed gratefully toward the bathroom, suddenly unable to wait a minute longer before taking my shower. I really hoped I could get the sour smoke smell out of my hair, or I was going to have to give myself a military buzz.

I was definitely planning to throw every piece of clothing I was wearing away.

The Hollows subdivision looked just like thousands of other new subdivisions across the country. It was being built on a few hundred acres of farmland, which was flat and unremarkable, with no trees or anything at all to break the monotony of ground and sky.

The Powers' lived on the main vein of the subdivision, the road to which all other crossroads and cul-de-sacs would one day be attached.

The homes were clearly starter homes, their metal siding broken only on the street-facing wall with faux brick or stone facades. Small trees of all the same size tipped slightly in every yard, clearly the victims of a driving wind that scoured the open land with not much to block it.

Most of the driveways held at least one car, which told me the homes probably didn't have basements and many of the garages were likely stuffed with items they couldn't store anyplace else.

All around us as we drove down Opossum Parkway was the evidence of young families, even, in a couple of cases, the actual children themselves playing busily behind pretty white picket fences. But the house we parked in front of had no toys. No car in the driveway, and nothing at all on the narrow front porch to suggest anyone ever used the exterior of the home.

We double-checked the numbers on the mailbox at the end of the drive. It was the right address. The one Deputy Craig had given us when Arno had made the request.

As we strode quickly toward the front door, my stomach growled enthusiastically. I covered it with my hand and felt my cheeks heat. "I should have had a snack at home before we left."

Hal grinned down at me. "This shouldn't take long. If I think she's our killer, I'm going to give her name to Arno for the deputies to pursue further."

I looked around the unassuming but comfortable neighborhood, letting the whole, "everyman" feeling infuse my cells. I found it really hard to believe that anyone who lived in that neighborhood, especially a woman who was probably in her early fifties, would drug a kind woman like Mary Willager and brutally stab a man to death.

But I'd certainly been surprised before.

Even by my own family.

The door opened after Hal knocked on it several times, and a woman with faded blonde hair and piercing gray eyes peered out at us. "Yes?"

Hal held up his private investigator's credentials.

"I'm Hal Amity and this is Joey Fulle. How are you today?"

She scowled at us over a pointy nose that pretty much dominated her narrow face. "I'm busy, and I don't like solicitors." She started to close the door, but Hal put out a hand. "Ma'am, I'm here at the behest of Deputy Willager. We have some questions for you. If you don't want to answer them here, we can go down to the station and you can answer them there."

His tone was firm but kind and the woman I assumed to be Samantha Powers seemed to understand it was in her best interests to cooperate. She stepped onto the porch, closing the door behind her as if she didn't want us to look inside. "What is this about?"

"Are you Samantha Powers?"

"I am. But I don't know anything about..."

"Do you know a man named Viper Branch?" Hal asked, interrupting her.

She fell silent, her mouth gaping open in surprise. Her close-set gray gaze slid to me as if she hoped I could help her understand what was going on.

I returned her stare and didn't say anything. Hal was more than capable of handling the interview with Ms. Powers. I didn't even know the woman so I'd be of no help at all.

"I...Yes. I knew him in high school. Why do you ask?"

"Are you aware that Mr. Branch was murdered?"

The woman's gaze slid to me again. She looked at Hal for a long moment and then gave a laughing response. "Seriously?"

"Yes, ma'am."

She shook her head, the grin remaining on her face. "Well, Praise the Lord."

"Excuse me?" Hal asked, clearly surprised by her response.

She laughed again. "Surely you don't expect me to mourn the monster who killed my dad?"

Hal stared at her, his expression neutral.

She leaned back against the closed door, crossing her arms over her chest. "You want to know if I killed him."

"Yes," Hal said. "Did you?"

"Unfortunately, no. But as you might have noticed, I'm not exactly broken up about it."

"Where were you around midnight on Tuesday night?"

"Midnight? Where everybody with half a brain should be. I was sleeping."

"Is there anyone who can corroborate that?"

She shook her head.

"No husband? Children?"

The woman turned defensive. "I'm single and

have no children, Mr. Amity. Does that instantly make me a suspect?"

He didn't bother responding to that one either. "Ms. Powers, what happened between you and Mr. Branch?"

She stared past us, her expression turning from belligerent to so sad it made me want to give her a hug. "He...pursued me in high school." After a moment during which she seemed to be casting her thoughts back to that time, she shook her head. "It wasn't genuine. Everyone knew he was incapable of caring for another human being. He liked to pretend he cared for people. And then when he'd drawn them in, he'd embarrass them in front of the other kids. I wasn't going to let him do that to me, and I told him as much. Several times. Finally, when I'd laid him out in front of the whole lunchroom, he coolly told me that I'd regret treating him that way. The next day my father was dead."

"You think Branch killed him?" I asked, letting my skepticism show.

Her face turned hard. "My parents were older. My dad was in his fifties when he got early-onset dementia. My mother and I cared for him and he was mostly doing well. But we had to keep him locked in at night, or he tended to wander the property. That night..." Samantha Powers struggled visibly with the memory and having to revisit it. "We found him floating in the pond. He couldn't have gotten outside by himself."

"You think Branch let him out of the house?"

She nodded. "It would have been easy to do. Daddy didn't sleep well, and he wandered the house most of the night. He liked to stand in front of the picture window in the living room. Anyone who was looking for him could have easily seen him there. All Branch had to do was find an unlocked window and come inside." She shuddered. "We found the open window the next morning. The screen was bent and crumpled on the ground outside." She wrapped her arms tightly around herself, sniffling. "Believe me, I wanted to kill him back then. In fact, I was so angry my mother insisted we move back to Indianapolis. She wanted me to start a new life. Let go of the rage."

"Did you do that?" I asked gently.

She nodded. "I did. But I never felt at home in Indy. So when mother died last year, I decided to come back to Deer Hollow."

"Why here?" Hal asked. "Why not some other small town where you didn't have such painful memories?"

She shrugged, her eyes filling with fresh tears. "I don't know. Deer Hollow is my home. I still have a few friends here. I was happy here before that monster ruined our lives. I thought I could be happy again."

11

We were eating our banana cream pie when Arno strode through the front door of Sonny's Diner. I could tell by the expression on his face that he didn't have good news for us.

Not that there was any good news to be had in the current mess.

He stopped beside the table and looked down at me. "Are you okay?"

I nodded, scooting over and patting the booth next to me for him to sit. "Any luck discovering who started the fire?"

Arno rubbed a hand over his face. "Nothing. It's like the guy's wearing an invisible suit. Not one person in the neighborhood saw anything strange. Including me and I was just next door."

Max rushed over with her order pad. "Deputy Willager. What can I get you?"

"Just coffee, please, Max. Thanks."

The waitress hurried away to get Arno's coffee, and Hal stood. "I'll be right back." I watched him walk over to Max and say something to her. She nodded, then they moved to the cash register.

He was paying our bill.

"You really should eat something, Arno," I said. "You look terrible."

He laughed bitterly. "Just what a guy wants to hear from an attractive woman."

I rubbed a hand over his back. "We're going to get to the bottom of this, Arno. Hal's good at what he does."

Arno nodded, looking up as Hal returned. "I wanted to tell you guys we got the results of mom's blood test and didn't see anything suspicious in it. Just her usual meds."

His gaze skimmed guiltily toward me, and he sighed. "I know I didn't answer your question before, Joey...about the dementia."

I nodded, waiting for him to go on.

"I've suspected something was wrong for a while now. She'd get confused over where she was and where she needed to go. She'd forget people's names. She's never forgotten names. My mother knows just about everybody in Deer Hollow. If she doesn't know them, she walks right up and introduces herself." He took a deep breath. "She's always been so sharp. But now..." His voice broke, and I rubbed his back again.

"Alzheimer's?" Hal asked softly.

Arno nodded. "Such a horrific disease." He looked at me, his eyes shiny. "She's only seventy-one."

Arno's mother had conceived him in her forties. He'd been the Willager's miracle child and they'd been thrilled to have him. But their age had ensured that he'd spent a lot more of his young life caring for his mother than the rest of his contemporaries.

I thought about Samantha Powers' story, my stomach clenching. "We actually just spoke to a woman...a potential suspect...whose father suffered from dementia." I didn't tell Arno how the man had ended up because it would scare him about his mom. "She believes Viper Branch killed him to spite her."

Arno's brows lifted. "That sounds like motive to me."

"We agree," Hal said. He skimmed me a look. "But I'm having trouble seeing Samantha Powers following us to Branch's house and flinging an explosive cocktail through the window."

"Could there be someone else who might be fighting her battle for her?" Arno asked. "A husband, maybe? An adult son?"

"She claims she never married or had children,"

I told him. "But it might be worth verifying. She could always have a boyfriend, I guess."

Arno nodded. We all glanced up when Max arrived with his coffee and a slice of pie. Arno opened his mouth to argue when she placed it in front of him, but Max shook her head. "It's paid for. Your friends think you need to eat something. I tend to agree with them." She squeezed his shoulder and turned away as tears filled Arno's eyes. "You guys have been amazing through all of this. I wanted to make sure I thanked you. My mind has been all over the place, and I'm likely to forget."

"We're glad to do it," I told him.

"We are," Hal agreed. "If there's anything else we can do don't hesitate to ask."

Arno gripped the heavy white mug, his jaw tightening. "I'm afraid I need to repay your kindness with distrust."

He looked up suddenly as if realizing how that had sounded. "Not my distrust. The Sheriff doesn't like that I've outsourced this to someone outside of the Sheriff's Department. I explained to him that, of the five men I currently have at my disposal, two are young and inexperienced in investigative work. One is dealing with some major health issues and just isn't dependable right now. And one is a week from retirement. Craig has no interest in digging into a murder investigation at this stage in his career."

"That's four," I said.

"I'm coming to that."

Hal and I shared a look. He frowned slightly, but I knew he wouldn't speak up. He'd respect their decision about our inclusion in the investigation without comment.

I'd known Arno too long to sit by and let us be railroaded, not after all the work we'd done. "We almost died today, Arno. We've made good progress."

He nodded, looking miserable. "I know. Believe me, I know. I argued with him until I was on the edge of losing my temper and doing something I'd regret."

"It's okay," Hal said. "We understand. We'll take our investigation into the shadows."

My gaze shot to Hal, and a smile tugged at my lips as he winked. Maybe he wasn't going to be as passive as I'd thought.

"That won't be necessary," Arno said. "I want you to have all the resources of the Sheriff's department at your disposal. I talked Sheriff Mulhern into letting you work with one of our guys."

I didn't like the sound of that, but it was better than being cut from the investigation. "Your fifth guy?"

Arno nodded. "There are reasons I didn't put this guy in charge in the first place. But I took a political risk doing it, and Sheriff Mulhern's been riding me for it."

"I take it that we're talking about someone who's connected to the Sheriff?" Hal asked.

"Nephew. Mark's not a bad guy, but he's a bit of a..." Arno's lips pinched together and he picked up his fork, slicing the tip off of his pie wedge. "I'll let you figure out what you've got. He'll be handy for doing things like running plates, getting addresses and priors from the database. But don't count on him to help you figure out who killed Viper Branch."

"We'll make it work," Hal said.

Arno stabbed the next bite before finishing the first. He swallowed and smiled. "You guys know me better than I know myself. I was apparently starving."

"Well, I mean, after all..." I said, grinning. "It is banana cream pie."

Arno stabbed another bite. He swallowed and grabbed his coffee, washing down the pie with a big swig. "Oh. That's good. I might live after all." He blinked, his own words apparently reminding him of something. "I keep forgetting to ask. How's the dog?"

"She's a little weak, but she's going to be okay," I said.

"Good. That's a relief. I'll tell mom. She's been worried. I called Doc Beetle this morning, but all I got was the clinical stuff, and that sounded dire."

"She's going to need TLC for a while," I agreed. "But she seems happy. And get this, LaLee even likes her."

He stabbed another bite, shaking his head. "Will wonders never cease?"

"Right?" I said. "If you'd like to see her with your own eyes, you can come to my house tonight for dinner. We're having steaks on the grill and salad. Nothing fancy."

He automatically started to shake his head at my invitation. As I'd known he would. "Lis is going to be there."

He didn't lift his gaze from his pie, but he stilled for a flicker in time. So quickly that I'd have missed it if I hadn't been looking for it. He still cared.

But he shook his head. "I can't. I have to stay on top of this."

"You need to eat, man," Hal said. "I'm sure your mom wouldn't want you sitting at your desk night and day."

"I'd feel guilty having fun while she's cooped up there."

"Just one hour. And we'll package up a go meal for your mom," I urged.

After another minute's hesitation, Arno finally nodded. "One hour." He stood up and looked at us for a long moment, his jaw tightening. He clearly wanted to say something but didn't appear to know how to say it. Finally, he nodded and turned toward the door, but not before throwing a last demand over his shoulder. "Come to the station in the morning, and I'll get you set up with Deputy Mark Sheppard."

We didn't make it out of Sonny's for a while. As we were preparing to leave, Verna Bly walked in, her apron thrown over one arm and her steps muted by her usual black orthopedic shoes. She turned a chilly gaze my way as we approached, her faded blue gaze tightening with pique. She reached up and extracted a pencil from her poufy, short black hair. "I hear y'all paid a visit to my husband. It would have been nice if you'd warned me."

I gave her an apologetic look. "I'm so sorry, Verna. We kind of decided in the spur of the moment to go have a chat."

"You think he killed Viper Branch?" she snipped.

Hal shook his head. "We just wanted to ask him some questions. It's part of the process. Arno asked us to help because, as you might have heard, his mother's right in the center of this mess."

Hal's carefully worded reminder of things beyond the Bly household worked perfectly. Verna's eyes lost some of their hostility. She popped her gum before nodding. "Yes. I have heard. There's no way Mary killed that enormous piece of dog poop. Though heaven knows he's given her plenty of reasons to over the years."

I looked around the room to make sure nobody was listening. The lunch hour was over and the place was mostly empty. Only the busboy, Jimmy Boston was even close, and he was far enough away that I didn't think he'd hear. "Verna, in your opinion, is it possible Mary was drugged or poisoned and didn't know what she was doing?" I asked softly.

Her eyes went wide. "Poisoned? Oh my. I don't know who would do such a thing."

"Maybe the person who killed Branch," Hal offered.

"How *was* Mary that night? You saw her at the flower committee meeting at the church, right?"

"I did." Verna frowned thoughtfully. "Now that you mention it, Mary did seem a little off. Kind of distracted or something. Old Mrs. Watson even asked her if she was feeling all right."

"How did Mary respond to that question?" Hal asked.

Verna shrugged. "She just kind of looked at the old busybody as if she couldn't quite remember who she was."

"Did Mary leave with everybody else," Hal asked?

"I can't remember. I was actually having a conversation with Samantha Powers about an arrangement we wanted to do for Fourth of July weekend. I think she might have walked out with Pastor Smythe that night."

After leaving Sonny's, we headed to Junior's to get food for dinner. I was perusing the salad options and Hal was selecting steaks in another part of the store when someone cleared their throat behind me.

I glanced over my shoulder and saw Reverend Smythe. He acted as if he'd only just spotted me. "Oh, hello, Joey! How nice to see you here."

"Hey, Reverend Smythe. How are you?"

"Oh, you know, keeping busy."

I got the distinct feeling he didn't want to engage in small talk, so I went back to my perusal of the lettuce options and waited for him to get to his point.

"I was wondering if you'd made any progress on the Branch murder?"

I dropped a bag of pre-washed romaine leaves into my cart and shook my head. "We seem to have more suspects than we know what to do with."

He sighed. "I was afraid of that. Did they..." His gaze flitted sideways, and I realized he was nervous. That was curious. "Was there anything found in those things you took from the church kitchen?"

"We haven't heard back on that yet," I told him. I leaned my arms on the handle of my cart and looked into his eyes. He shuffled his feet slightly. "What's bothering you, Reverend Smythe?"

He jerked his head in the negative as if considering denying my suggestion, but then he sighed. "I wasn't entirely truthful with you and Mr. Amity. I'm deeply sorry about that."

"You mean about your wife?"

His face paled to the color of chalk. "You know about that?"

"Things tend to come out when you talk to a lot of people."

He nodded, his age-speckled hands twining nervously together. "I really didn't think it was important. I assure you I didn't kill that man."

I cocked my head. "You realize that, by lying, you make yourself look guilty."

He sighed. "Yes. That's why I wanted to come clean. I'll admit I did hold a lot of anger after she left me. Any man would. But I've prayed on it for countless hours, and I've put it behind me."

"If that's true, why do you think you neglected to tell us about it," I asked.

He shrugged. "Pride. I know it's a sin, but I have enough pride that I didn't want to air that dirty laundry again, especially in front of you young people. It's embarrassing to have lost the woman I loved to a man like Viper Branch."

I could certainly understand that. "There's something else maybe you could help us with. Hal and I have a witness who claimed you walked out of the flower committee meeting with Mary Willager on the night of the murder. Is that true?"

"Why, yes, I believe I did. To be honest, she

seemed a little off, and I was afraid she'd have trouble getting to her car. I offered her a ride, but she just smiled at me the way she does and said she'd be fine. She said she had to make a stop on the way home."

That was news. "You didn't tell us that before either," I scolded gently.

The pastor looked ashamed. "I didn't think of it until just now. I'm sorry."

I watched him walk away, my mind sliding back over our initial conversation with the pastor. I remembered the look on his face as he walked away. He'd looked upset about something. Knowing what I knew now, I assumed he was bothered by the fact that he hadn't told us everything he knew.

But given all the other information he'd also left out, I returned to my original thought. I couldn't help wondering if Reverend Smythe was still holding something back.

$\mathcal{D}$eputy Mark Sheppard was probably the smallest man I'd ever met. At five feet four, I stood head to head with the man and I was pretty sure my arms were bigger around than his legs. It wasn't often I felt like a giant around somebody, especially not a man. But standing next to Sheppard, I was kind of feeling like I should be wearing a loincloth and chucking spears at my enemies.

Hal stood next to me, looking down at the diminutive deputy like he wasn't sure we were meeting the right guy.

Arno stood behind Sheppard with his arms crossed over his chest, his face a neutral mask.

For his part, Sheppard seemed blissfully unaware that he was barely taller than a healthy ten-year-old. In fact, the way he was strutting around the office, making wholly unnecessary copies of the "report" he'd "worked up" on the murder in an attempt to "get us up to speed" it was clear the deputy thought he was "all that" and more.

Much more.

He tapped the edges of the pile of paper on the surface of his desk and grabbed the stapler. "This will help you understand the players in the investigation. I know some of the lingo will be hard for you to grasp, given that you're laypeople and all..."

Hal's gaze lifted to Arno, and he arched a brow.

Arno seemed to be fighting to keep from laughing.

Seeing no help at all from that quarter, Hal offered Sheppard a smile. "You know I was a cop for ten years in Indianapolis, right?"

Sheppard's return smile dripped with condescension. "I'm sure you did a fine job," he said, handing Hal the pile of paper, which had three staples in one corner, each one even less effective than the last. As Hal took the stack, two of the staples rained down onto his shoe like pointy metal snowflakes. "And I'll just take your word for it that you left of your own volition," Sheppard said as he reached out and patted Hal on the arm. "Not everyone is cut out for police work. I'm sure you did your best."

I coughed into my hand as Hal turned pink and then red.

At that point, Arno, being a smart man whose skills reading people were fortunately much better than Sheppard's, stepped forward. "Deputy Sheppard will be your liaison here at the Sheriff's office. If you wouldn't mind bringing him up to speed with what you've found so far...?" He eyed Hal until my PI nodded.

"Of course."

Arno's words slipped off Sheppard as if he'd just emerged from a vat of oil. He pointed to the two hard, wood chairs which sat on the opposite side of his tidy desk. "Have a seat. We can go over my report together."

Arno slipped away as Sheppard smoothed out the top sheet of his pile of paper and looked down at it, his shoulders squaring as he began to read. "On May twenty-first, two thousand nineteen, one Viper Branch of Twenty-five Sixteen Antler's Way was found deceased, with several wounds upon his chest and extremities that seemed to suggest a sharp blade of some kind was used on him."

Hal glanced my way, his gaze filled with despair, and mouthed, *do something* as Sheppard continued to drone on. I barely fought off a grin, knowing my good humor would be short-lived if we had to sit there and listen to Sheppard read the entirety of his "report" to us.

Ayn Rand had nothing on this guy. He might be short in stature, but he was long on words. "Um,

Deputy Sheppard," I said with a harmless-looking smile. "You're right. This is a lot of information. I wonder if it would be okay if we looked it over later? I'd like to run some things past you and get your opinion."

I added just the right mix of overwhelmed and confused to my delivery that he would have seemed like a cad if he'd bowled me over. Besides, I was just living down to his low opinion of me. He puffed his small chest and nodded, rubbing a hand over the pile of paper as if he was so grateful to it for showing him what we were made of.

Or to be more accurate, what we *weren't* made of.

"Of course. As I said, I know this can be overwhelming to someone who doesn't understand police work."

Hal gave up trying not to roll his eyes. Fortunately, Sheppard was distracted looking for something in his center drawer. He dug around for a moment and then came up with a pen, sliding the drawer closed. He pushed his report to the side, neatly adjusting it so that it was perfectly square with the edges of the desk, and then pulled a lined note pad out of a wire basket on the top left corner of the desk.

He arranged it on the desk and poised his pen over it, looking expectantly at Hal. "Mr. Amity, would you like to begin?"

Hal's eyes seemed to want to roll again, but I

reached over and pinched his thigh, getting a glare for my trouble. "Um, sure. Joey and I have isolated several suspects during the investigation so far..."

Sheppard started to write a title for his notes across the top of the page. He managed to carefully form the letters, List of Sus... before his pen dried up. He breathed on the tip and then scratched it over a yellow stickie pad, to no avail. He glanced up, sliding the center drawer open again. "Sorry." After another moment's digging, he unearthed a second pen, dropping the dried-up pen back into the drawer.

I was thinking we might have identified the problem.

Sheppard started to complete the word "Suspect" but couldn't get the "p" to line up with the rest of the word, so he tore that sheet off the pad and crumpled it up, flinging it toward the trash can by the wall.

He of course missed and had to get up and retrieve the ball of paper, dropping it into the trash before returning to his desk.

Hal shifted in the hard chair, and I coughed to cover the laugh bubbling in my throat.

Sheppard wrote, List of Susp... And the second pen dried up.

He breathed on the tip, scratched it across a fresh stickie, and then looked up with an apologetic smile. "Sorry..."

He pulled open the center drawer...

Hal's hand flashed out and yanked the pen from Sheppard, breaking it in half and flinging both halves toward the trash can across the room.

Both pieces made it into the container.

"Why don't we do a verbal report first. You can type it up later," Hal said through gritted teeth.

Sheppard frowned.

I suspected he was concerned about changing his process. But Hal wasn't waiting any longer.

"As I said, we have a list..." He stopped, his gaze sliding to the unfinished word on Sheppard's pad, and Shepard's gaze followed suit.

Hal quickly adjusted. "We've identified several people who had motive to kill the victim."

Sheppard opened his mouth, but Hal bowled him over. "Our initial witness/person of interest is Mary Willager. Aside from being found at the scene of the murder, holding the murder weapon in her hand, she had opportunity, means, and potential motive, though we haven't verified that Branch actually poisoned her dog. That's on the To-Do list."

Sheppard nodded, glancing down at his pad as his expression tightened. His fingers twitched toward the center drawer, but Hal gave him stink eye and he stilled. "Um, yes, go on," Sheppard said, clearing his throat nervously.

"We believe Mary Willager might be suffering from dementia or was dosed with something to impair her memory. She seems to have no recollection of how she ended up next to the body holding a knife."

Sheppard didn't look convinced of Mary's memory loss, but he shrugged and said nothing.

"We also learned that Reverend Smythe at the Lutheran Church has motive and he had opportunity to dose Mary Willager if that's what occurred. He lost his wife to the victim and had witnessed Branch's cruelty to animals and people first hand."

Sheppard's fingers clenched and unclenched over his pad until he forced them into fists and jammed them into his pockets, leaning back in his chair. He was so upset about not being able to write things down on his pad of paper, I wasn't sure he was even hearing what Hal was saying.

"Next, we have Samantha Powers. She's recently returned to Deer Hollow after a long absence and was at the same flower committee meeting at the Lutheran Church that night as Mary Willager. Ms. Powers blames Branch for the death of her father, who suffered from dementia and was prone to wandering. She believes Branch released the senior Mr. Powers from a locked home one night as retribution for her rejecting his advances. Mr. Powers ended up drowning in the family pond that night. Ms. Powers has no alibi for the night in question. She had motive, potentially the means, and opportunity."

Despite himself, Sheppard was getting interested. He tugged his fists from his pockets and
leaned forward, focusing on Hal's recital.

"Then we have Robert Bly, who had a public
altercation with the victim last month at Mabel's Bar
and Grill over damage done to Bly's restored
Mustang. Bly had motive, the same means as
everyone else, and his only alibi is his wife." Hal
took a deep breath. "Next we have..."

Sheppard looked flabbergasted. "There are more
suspects? How is that possible?"

I gave him a sad smile. "I'm afraid Viper Branch
was almost universally hated."

The deputy shook his head. "We're going to need
a really big murder board for this one."

Hal apparently decided not to touch that one. He
continued where he'd left off. "...Nancy Villa, whose
car the neighbor saw heading toward Mary's home
right after Mary left for a meeting Mrs. Villa was
aware she attended."

Sheppard nodded thoughtfully.

"Though we've isolated no motive for Mrs. Villa
and she has no real alibi for the time of the
murder, we're keeping her on the list because she
potentially had the means to grab a knife from
Mary's kitchen. Though it should be noted that she
denies being in the vicinity on the day of the
murder. She says she was sick, a fact that we intend
to verify by speaking to her cousin, Betty Weldt,

who apparently brought Nancy chicken noodle soup."

I sat miserable and mute during Hal's coldly analytical verbalizing of Nancy's spot on our list. I realized he needed to consider her because she'd been at the wrong place at the wrong time. But I couldn't help thinking that, if Lis's mom *did* turn out to be a strong suspect, Lis would probably never speak to me again. I sighed.

"Finally, we have George Shulz. Deer Hollow's only resident lawyer. Aside from being almost universally hated himself, Shulz was working with Branch on a business item and made regular visits to Branch's home, which I can say from direct experience is an odd occurrence."

Sheppard shrugged, offering an opinion in the form of a disbelieving tone to his question. "He's a suspect because he made house calls?" The deputy frowned, clearly not impressed by that bit of reasoning.

Hal shook his head. "He's a suspect because he's...him. And because his behavior is out of character, which means it's worth taking a careful look at."

Sheppard shrugged, looking slightly petulant. I figured he was getting irritated that we had, in fact, done quite a bit of legwork. He'd probably been telling himself he'd have to whip the two pretend cops into shape before he quickly solved the case.

"And as a general point of consideration," Hal continued after sliding me a quick look, "we need to look at Branch's blog for sociopaths."

Sheppard blinked at that. "Blog for what, now?"

Hal leaned over the desk, grabbed the pen that had been resting against Sheppard's blotter the entire time he'd been digging for another one, and quickly jotted the URL down on a stickie. "Check it out."

I pressed my lips together as Sheppard eyed the pen Hal dropped in front of him, clearly annoyed he'd missed it earlier.

That pen had worked just fine.

The deputy typed the URL into his laptop and started reading, his slightly bulging gaze widening with every paragraph.

"That blog would have alienated every woman in Deer Hollow who read it," I offered as Sheppard's mouth fell open. "Which, I think you'd agree, vastly increases our suspect pool."

Sheppard ripped his gaze from the computer screen. He thought about what I'd said and then shook his head, dismissing it. "Not everyone would have had means. We've identified the murder weapon as having come directly from Mary Willager's kitchen. She has one of those butcher block knife holder things and the murder weapon was missing from its slot."

"Yes," Hal said agreeably, which should have

been warning enough for Deputy Sheppard. "From a kitchen in a house whose door is never locked. It was common knowledge that Mary didn't lock her house up during the day. And in a town as small as Deer Hollow, her whereabouts would also be generally known. Anyone who knew that Mary took a walk every morning at six AM or went to a meeting at the church every Tuesday evening at five would have been able to grab that knife, making means a pretty global thing."

"And motive is only slightly less global," I added. "Nearly everyone hated Viper Branch. He'd alienated, harmed or just generally hacked off everybody we've talked to, suspect or not."

Sheppard's face fell. Watching his narrow shoulders slump, I almost felt bad for taking the starch from the cocky deputy's sails.

Almost.

"Well then, it looks like you've focused on the reasons why we *can't* find the killer. But that's not very productive. I guess it'll be up to me to figure out who the killer is," Sheppard said, regaining some of the starch he'd lost as he re-squared his shoulders.

I looked at Hal, expecting him to bristle at the unveiled criticism. Instead, I was shocked to see him smile. "You're absolutely right, Sheppard, which is why I bow to you to do the murder board. I think it will be an invaluable exercise in discovering our killer."

My lips twitched as I realized what he'd done.

Sheppard's chest puffed, his expression regaining its smug aspect. He nodded. "I believe you're right, Mr. Amity." He stood up and magnanimously offered Hal a hand that was only slightly bigger than mine. "It takes a big man to admit when he's out of his league."

Though Hal's jaw tightened and he looked at the hand a beat too long, he finally took it and gave it one small jerk before dropping it. "Deputy." Hal nodded and turned toward me, jerking his head toward the hallway leading to Arno's office. "Shall we go say hello to Mary while we're here?"

"Um, yes. Let's," I stammered out. Just when I thought my PI couldn't amaze me any more with his good sense and patience, he took an ineffectual hit on the square jaw from a bug with a badge and turned the other cheek in the best interests of solving the case.

Despite the gargantuan unfairness of having his detecting skills insulted by a man who couldn't find his own pen when it was sitting eight inches away on top of his desk.

$\mathcal{I}$ was chopping cucumbers, fending off a pushy pibl and keeping an eye on my sleeping patient, when Hal called. I made a grab for my cell phone, knocking a chunk of cucumber onto the floor where it was immediately tackled into submission and snarfed up in one bite. I shook my head at Caphy and punched the button to answer Hal's call. "Hey!"

"Hey, yourself. I wanted to let you know I'm bringing some wine."

"Oh, good. Lis is bringing some too, but she and I will probably plow through those pretty fast."

He chuckled. "Good thing we have beer for Arno and me then."

"Yeah," I grinned, following Caphy's lead and popping a slice of cucumber into my mouth. "When are you coming?"

"I'm on my way now."

"Good."

Silence pulsed between us, and I stopped chopping to pay closer attention. Hal had something he wanted to tell me but he knew I wasn't going to like it. "What is it?"

"Is Lis there?"

"Not yet." I frowned, not liking the question. "Why?"

"Sheppard just called me."

Oh, oh. "Okay."

"It appears he's not quite as clueless as he seems."

My stomach twisted with alarm. "You're scaring me, Hal. Just spit it out."

He sighed. "Sheppard visited Nancy Villa today and asked her if he could check her Navigational software."

A lump tightened my throat. "Okay. I'm guessing you're going to tell me she went somewhere she shouldn't have?"

"I don't' know about that, Joey. But we do now have proof that she went to see Mary the evening of the murder." He hesitated for a beat and then, in case I didn't catch what he was throwin' said, "She lied to us, Joey."

I'm pretty sure my heart stopped beating. I stood rigidly, dread making it hard to breathe. Something warm and soft pressed against my leg, and I looked down, expecting to see Caphy.

Spunky's sweet, graying face stared up at me, her thick fringe of a tail whipping the air behind her. She licked my hand, her brown eyes locked onto my face.

I dropped to my knees and buried my face in her soft fur.

"Joey?" Hal sounded worried at my silence.

"I'm here."

"I'm sorry, honey."

I swallowed hard. "I'm sure there's an innocent reason for it," I told him, praying it was true.

There was a beat of silence before he answered. "I'm sure you're right. I'll see you in two minutes, okay?"

Caphy suddenly jumped up from the spot where she was sprawled. She took off running toward the front door. And my heart twisted. Lis had arrived. I suddenly couldn't face her. Panicking, I considered telling her I didn't feel well and canceling.

That would be cowardly.

But I wasn't above cowardly.

Caphy's happy greeting sounds turned a bit less happy, and I heard the distinctive sound of her heavy body slamming against the front door and then her low growl.

To my shock, Spunky took off running to the front door too.

I hurried after her, no longer worried about Lis. Now I was concerned about who else might have arrived.

Caphy ran to the living room window and jumped up, her paws resting on the sill as she pressed her face against the glass, adding new smears to the ones she'd put there when the delivery man had arrived earlier with a package.

I don't know why I even bothered cleaning it.

Spunky stood back from the door, her big body rigid. To my shock, she was growling low and deep in her throat, her tail tucked.

I put a hand on her head. "What is it, girl?" She didn't look at me, but she pressed against my leg, her tail giving a single wag. And when I tried to step closer to the door, she moved to get in my way. "Spunky..."

Something slammed into the door and I jumped, yelping in fear and surprise as Spunky took off. The two dogs met at the door, both of them growling and barking, their faces pressed close to the crack between the door and the frame.

I moved quickly to the window in the living room, keeping to one side as I tried to peer outside.

That was when I realized the porch light was off. I'd left it on earlier for my guests so it shouldn't be off. I frowned, not liking the chances that was just a harmless coincidence.

Something swept over the window, and I jumped

back with a scream. The dogs threw themselves at the door, barking frantically.

My cell rang and I twitched with nerves, looking down to see Lis's name on the screen. I hit *Ignore* and dialed Hal instead. He answered as a set of headlights hit my driveway. "Hey, did you forget something?"

"Hal," I said in a harsh whisper. "Somebody's here."

"What? I can't hear you with all the barking. What's wrong with the dogs?"

I moved away from the window, ready to fling the door open once Hal pulled up to the steps. "Somebody's here!" I said loudly. "The dogs are freaking out."

"Stay inside. I'm pulling up now."

His headlights danced across the window in the living room. Caphy started to run in that direction but I grabbed her collar before she could. "No, baby girl. We're staying right here until Hal comes to the door."

I waited, barely breathing as footsteps sounded on the porch. The dogs watched the door, heads cocked as they listened.

A moment later a soft knock had me starting with nerves.

"Joey? It's me."

I hurried to unlock the front door and Caphy

charged through, jumping up to lavish Hal with kisses.

He didn't smile at her antics. In fact, the light from the entryway bathed his concerned face and wary gaze. "Call Arno."

I frowned. "Arno? Why?"

He stepped forward as I tried to come through the door, keeping a hand on Caphy's collar and pushing her into the house as he came. "Please, just do it, Joey."

Icy fingers slipped down my spine from the look on his face. "Tell me." It wasn't a request. Hal seemed to recognize the panic behind the words because he relented. "I don't want you to go outside."

"What? You're scaring me, Hal."

"Good. You need to be scared. Call Arno."

His cold, brusque manner got through to me where nothing else could. I quickly dialed Arno's number and waited, my gaze locked on Hal's.

He stood in front of the door, scratching the dogs' ears. The two canines acted as if nothing was amiss, which told me whoever had been outside my house was gone.

So why was Hal so intense?

"Willager."

"Arno, I need you to come out to my house right away."

"Joey, I know I told you I'd come to dinner but..."

"No," I cut him off. "This isn't about dinner. Something's happened."

"What's happened? Are you okay? Lis?"

My eyes flew wide. "Lis?!" I asked Hal, panicking.

Hal shook his head, taking the phone from my hand and opening the door. He threw me a look before going out to talk to Arno in secret. "Call her and tell her not to come." Then he closed the door and I heard the deep rumble of his voice on my porch.

I sagged in relief, able to breathe again. Lis was okay. Whatever had Hal spooked, it wasn't her. Hurrying into the kitchen, I grabbed the landline phone. I dialed her number and got her voicemail. I left a quick message telling her that dinner was canceled and that I'd call later to explain, and then hung up, hoping she wasn't already on her way.

The dogs sat in front of the door, whining softly. I wanted to whine too. It wasn't fair for Hal to keep me in the dark. So when Arno's car hit my driveway, lights flashing but sirens silent, I grabbed a flashlight and opened the door, stepping out onto my porch.

Hal was waiting for Arno in the circular drive. He turned as I came through the door but he didn't say anything. I was pretty sure he'd known I wouldn't stay in the house.

He came up the steps as I offered him the flashlight.

"I thought you might want to see what you were doing out here."

He sighed, taking the flashlight from my hand. The dogs skipped past us and headed out to greet Arno as he stopped the Sheriff's cruiser next to Hal's car.

He left the lights on and climbed out of his car, standing next to it and staring up at my house. "Crap!" he said, his face bathed in the red and blue flashing lights.

Curious about his reaction, I turned and gasped, backpedaling until I came up against Hal. My heart was pounding so hard I could barely hear what Arno was saying as he approached.

Spunky lumbered slowly back up the steps and sat down beside me, whining softly.

My hand dropped automatically to rest on her soft head, and she shoved it against my hand, distracting me enough that I was able to look away from the horror jutting from my front door.

"Did you see him?" Arno asked as he stopped next to Hal.

Hal looked at me. "I don't think Joey did. By the time I got here he was gone."

Arno turned to me. My gaze slid to his, no doubt filled with the horror turning my spine to ice. "Joey?"

I swallowed the lump in my throat and managed to shake my head. "There was a loud thump and the dogs came running." I shook my head, helpless to stop my mind from taking me back to the terror of that moment. "I wouldn't let them go outside. I could tell by their reaction that it wasn't someone they trusted."

Arno nodded, glancing toward Hal.

Hal took whatever cue Arno sent him with that look and reached for me, wrapping me in his arms and turning me away from the door. "Let's step away and let Arno do his work, okay?"

I resisted being drawn toward the house. "No. I want to stay out here. I'll go crazy in there."

Hal nodded. "No problem. We'll just go down by my car, okay?"

I nodded, letting him lead me away. Arno followed.

"Did you see who did this, Joey?"

I shook my head. "I tried looking out the window but..." I shuddered, remembering. "Whoever was there, saw me and did something to the window." I turned to look at the dark rectangle of glass, seeing the gentle, welcoming light of the entryway beyond the panes. And something else, which I couldn't identify in the dark.

I grabbed the flashlight from Hal and shone it over the window. Gasping, I stumbled forward in shock. "Is that blood?"

"It looks that way," Arno said, sighing. "I'm pulling you off this investigation."

My head was shaking before Hal even started to

argue. "Not a chance, Arno. I'm not going to let this bully win."

"Joey, you have a meat cleaver stuck to your front door that somebody used as an oversized tack to pin a message warning you to mind your own business," Arno said.

"And blood painted across the front of your house," Hal added.

"This is not something you can just shrug off," Arno finished.

"He's right, Joey. You need to step away from this. I'll handle it from here on out. You trust me, don't you?"

Dang him for making it about trust. That was a dirty trick. I frowned. "Of course, I trust you. I trust both of you. That's not what this is about. I'm not going to let someone chase me away. They don't get to win."

"Joey, if the killer makes good on this threat, we're going to be the ones who lose," Hal said, his voice breaking.

His emotion touched me. I reached out and took his hand. "Hal, there's no guarantee that whoever this is will walk away from this threat anyway. I won't be safe until this guy's in jail. You know that's true."

I could tell from the look on his face that I was right "I'll compromise. The animals and I will come stay with you until this is over."

His eyes went wide and he appeared to pale,

though that could have been an effect of the flashing lights. Mm-hm. "Even LaLee?" His voice broke slightly on the cat's name. I grinned. "You don't want her to be in danger, do you?"

He actually had to think about that for a minute. In fact, he thought about it until I punched his arm. "No, of course not," he finally said. Though his expression made me seriously doubt his sincerity.

"Good," Arno said. "I'll get a team out here to process this. The sooner you can vacate the premises the better."

I sighed. "I'll pack a bag."

"Before you do," Arno said. His expression turned grim. "I spoke to Doc Beetle today. He's finally identified the poison Spunky ingested."

"Really?" Hal asked, his interest clear. "Hopefully, it's something rare enough that it will help us identify a killer."

"I wish," Arno said, sighing. "It's not only *not* rare, it's actually pretty common, and readily available enough that Spunky could have actually poisoned herself."

14

"So, what is it?" I asked. I glanced down at the dogs. Spunky was pressed against my left hip while Caphy pressed against my right. Caphy jittered and twitched, a goofy look on her sweet face. Spunky smiled up at me, her eyes sparkling with affection. I couldn't believe anyone would try to hurt such a sweet dog. But, then again, maybe Arno's suggestion would turn out to be the truth. Maybe she'd accidentally poisoned herself.

"Rhododendron."

Hal and I stared at him. Finally, I said. "You mean, like the flower?"

Arno nodded. "It's toxic to dogs if they consume it."

"Does your mother have that flower around her house?" Hal asked.

"That's just the thing..." Arno said, frowning, "I don't think she does. At least, she didn't as of last summer. I remember her remarking about a neighbor's bushes, saying she'd never have a rhododendron because they were toxic to dogs."

"Could Spunky have chewed on the neighbor's bush?" I asked.

"It's possible. But not likely. Because of Branch's hostility and threats, mom keeps Spunky close." He looked down at the big retriever, a soft light filling his eyes. "She's much too smart to wander off the property." He knelt down, framing Spunky's muzzle with his hands and scratching under her ears. "Aren't you, girl?"

The dog's eyes narrowed to slits and one of her back legs kicked toward her belly with pleasure.

We all chuckled.

"You said one of the neighbors had a bush," Hal said. "Do you know which one?"

Arno straightened back up, frowning. "I'm pretty sure it's the big house on the same side of the street as mom's house."

"On the other side of Branch's house?"

Arno nodded. "I think that's the one. Though it's set pretty far back from the road, so I'm not sure. I can verify that with mom."

"That would be great, thanks," Hal said.

But I realized it wouldn't be necessary as a

memory resurfaced. "I don't think you need to do that, Arno."

When he looked at me, I glanced toward Hal. "Ginnie Weldt was trimming a rhododendron bush when we spoke to her."

"That huge bush with the pink flowers?" he asked.

I nodded. Looking at Arno, I asked. "What do you know about Ginnie Weldt?"

"Not much. Everybody on mom's street pretty much keeps to themselves. Probably because of Branch. Nobody wanted to risk hacking him off." Arno shook his head. "I should have found a reason to put him in jail years ago." His gaze slid to Spunky again, turning speculative.

"Ginnie told us she lost her husband several months ago," Hal offered.

"Yeah. There was nothing hinky about his death though, if that's what you're suggesting."

"Anything else that might give her motive to kill Branch?" Hal asked.

"Not that I'm aware of, no." Arno glanced over his shoulder as two more Sheriff's vehicles pulled into my drive. "You might want to send Sheppard over to talk to Mrs. Weldt. I'll talk to Mom about her neighbors as soon as we're done here and let you know what I find out."

"Thanks, Arno." I gave him a smile and was

happy to see him return it. He seemed to have calmed down a bit from the night of the murder. The night he'd had to arrest his own mother for murder. Then I understood why. The attacks on Hal and I had gone a long way toward proving that Mary wasn't our killer. That realization *almost* put a smile on my face. "I'll just go grab some things for me and the dogs," I told Hal as Arno descended the steps to meet the other deputies.

Hal nodded absently, watching the men climb out of their squad cars.

When I came out a few minutes later, carrying LaLee in one hand and a duffle bag in the other, Hal was closing the back of the big SUV and the dogs were bouncing around inside, making the car bobble.

He took the bag from me. "Hey, cat."

LaLee hissed at him and he promptly sneezed.

I eyed him, wondering if his cat allergies might be more emotional than physical. We climbed into the car. "I was thinking that maybe we should check Branch's garage for rhododendron cuttings or something."

"You're thinking he might have bought a plant just to poison Spunky?"

"It's possible, right? At least we can mark him off the list of potential dog poisoners if there's nothing there."

Hal nodded. "Maybe."

He was quiet on the way to his cabin and as we got the animals settled. By the time we climbed back into his car to make the trek to Branch's house, I was really starting to get concerned. "What's bothering you?" I asked.

He looked at me in surprise. "Nothing. Why do you ask?"

I gave him a look and he sighed. "I'm just worried about you. Whoever we're chasing has proven himself to be ruthless. I don't know what I'd do if something happened to you."

Tears burned my gaze and I leaned across the car, kissing him on the cheek before resting my head on his shoulder. "I'm going to be fine. I'm not exactly helpless, you know. And I have you, two dogs and a killer cat to protect me."

Hal chuckled. "I'm not sure about the dogs. They might just try to lick the killer to death. But LaLee, now she might come in handy in a life or death battle."

Thinking of all the times Caphy had flown into battle to protect me, and how Spunky had stepped in front of me to keep me away from the front door, I doubted Hal's assessment of them was right. But I understood his concerns.

"We'll just have to find the real killer," I told him, my tone filled with much more confidence than I felt. "Then we'll all be safe and there will be nothing to worry about anymore."

He nodded but remained thoughtful for the rest of the drive. Ten minutes later we pulled down Antler's Way and Hal parked the Escalade in the driveway of Branch's house. We stepped out and stood, looking up and down the short residential street.

Arno's words about everyone keeping to themselves resurfaced as I found myself looking at one after another empty front yard.

Hal headed for the free-standing garage. It was a ramshackle wood building that had been painted white once, probably a long time ago. The end closest to where the house had been was lightly scorched, but the fire department had managed to keep it mostly intact. The front doors of the building were chained together but the smaller side door was unlocked. The window in the side door was broken, probably from the heat of the fire.

I kept my gaze averted from the reddish-brown stains where Branch's body had been, and followed Hal around to the side.

Hal pushed the door open and my nose twitched as a wave of mildewy air assaulted me.

He sneezed, grimacing. "Leave the door open until I find a light switch," he instructed.

Naturally, the switch wasn't located on the wall nearest the door. That would make too much sense.

"I'm for leaving it open anyway," I said, covering my face with my hand. "it stinks in here."

Hal's big shoe splashed down on the floor as he headed for a bare bulb in the center of the building. "I'm guessing this water is from the fire. They probably doused the building to keep it from catching." He tugged the string hanging from the bulb and light flared into the space. It wasn't enough to illuminate the whole building, but it did bring most of the center into view.

A red Jeep Wrangler occupied most of the open area in the center. The walls were covered in wood shelving hung from heavy-duty shelving supports that were attached to the exposed framing. The shelves were covered in tools, car care stuff, and lawn care equipment. I saw no gardening tools, which didn't surprise me since I just couldn't see Branch planting and tending flowers or trees.

I walked along the wall, eyeing the overflowing shelves and thinking it was amazing how many tools a man could collect in the off chance he might someday need them.

"Rat poison."

I turned and looked at Hal, who was checking out the shelves on the other side of the garage. I grimaced. "I'm glad he didn't use that on poor Spunky." But my traitorous mind couldn't help wondering if Branch had used it on anybody else's beloved pet.

We met in the middle, in front of a pile of lumber and wood scraps, a stack of roofing tiles, and a wheelbarrow filled with old tires.

"No rhododendron," Hal said. "Let's get out of here before my lungs seize up."

I nodded. "You don't have to ask me twice."

We walked down to Ginnie Weldt's house and knocked on her door. She didn't answer and, after a moment, we gave up. I wandered over to the giant rhododendron bush, rubbing a finger over a freshly cut branch. "All it would have taken is a single cutting," I said to Hal. "I don't know how we'd know if it came from here."

He nodded, looking thoughtful. "Let's go talk to Doc Beetle. Maybe he can tell us something he didn't think to tell Arno."

I thought that sounded like a great idea and followed him to the Escalade, climbing in as depression nudged at my psyche. It was looking more and more as if Nancy Villa had the best opportunity to kill Branch. And she'd lied to us about being there that day. But we still had no idea why she'd want him dead. Aside from the obvious.

"What are you thinking about?"

I shrugged, then sighed as Hal gave me a look that told me he wasn't going to give up until I spilled. "Okay, I was just thinking about Nancy Villa. I know it looks bad..."

He nodded. "It does. But we don't have motive yet."

"How are we going to get that?" I asked, fighting back tears.

"One step at a time. Let's talk to Doc first. Then we'll go talk to Betty about her cousin. She'll know if Nancy had anything against Branch."

I felt better having a plan that didn't include directly accusing Nancy of murder. "Yeah. That makes sense."

Doc was sitting at Sally's desk when we came through the door. He looked up in surprise, glancing at his watch. "Joey, we didn't have an appointment, did we?"

"No. Hal and I just wanted to ask you a few questions about Spunky. If you don't mind."

He scrawled a signature over a form and laid the pen down on top of it, shoving back from the desk and nodding. "Go ahead. I was just about to head out for some lunch before my afternoon appointments start arriving."

"We'll make it quick, sir," Hal told him. "Arno told us you believed Spunky was poisoned by rhododendrons?"

Doc shook his head. "That boy doesn't know if he's coming or going these days. That's technically but not specifically correct. She suffered from grayanotoxin poisoning. Grayanotoxins are prevalent in some forms of rhododendron and the honey made from the flowers can be highly toxic."

"I don't understand," Hal said. "If the honey is toxic, why would someone eat it?"

"They call it Mad Honey because of its hallucinogenic properties. But, in the right amounts, the honey is also good for treating hypertension, diabetes and stomach diseases, and it has antiviral and antibacterial properties."

Doc's words flipped a switch in my memory and my heart sped up. "So, you believe someone fed Spunky this Mad Honey?"

Doc Beetle frowned. "All I know is that she suffered the classic symptoms of grayanotoxin poisoning and that there was a sticky substance around her muzzle that I was able to identify as honey under the microscope."

"Thanks, Doc," Hal said. "You've been very helpful."

The veterinarian stood, tugging his slacks up over his round belly. "I can also tell you that the honey was not mass-produced. It would have been homemade or manufactured in a small, organic facility."

"How do you know that?" I asked.

"Because of the amount of pollen in the sample. Large-scale manufacturing removes much of the pollen when they develop honey. Whoever harvested this honey is selling it in a virtually raw state."

As we walked out of Doc's I looked at Hal. "We need to go talk to Betty."

He nodded. "You read my mind."

15

_I_t's fascinating how perception changes as you grow older. When I was eight years old and visiting Betty's farm with Lis, I thought it was an enormous place filled with wonders and magic.

Now, twenty years later, I realized that, while the Weldt farm still might be filled with wonders and magic, the house at least was really just a normal, sprawling farmhouse that had been added onto several times throughout the years.

Painted an unexceptional white with black shutters, the farmhouse was slightly careworn around the edges, but seemed mostly well-maintained.

A three-wheeled motorcycle was parked in the gravel in front of the house.

The barn in the distance was a faded red, its doors crisscrossed with white and hay spilling from the loft window in the peak. I smiled fondly at the sight of that window, remembering all the hours of fun Lis and I had spent in that hayloft, pretending.

Hal stopped the car and we started to climb out. But Hal's phone rang and we stopped.

"Amity," he answered. He listened for a moment and then turned to roll his eyes at me. "Hello, Deputy."

Judging by the eye-rolling exercise, I figured it was Sheppard rather than Arno.

"We're getting ready to interview someone about a potential suspect."

His words made my stomach twist and I took a deep breath, trying to calm my nerves.

"Yes? No kidding? Okay, we'll stop in after we speak to Ms. Weldt. Okay. Yeah, thanks."

"What did he want?" I asked, my hand still on the door handle.

"He's been doing a deep dive into Branch's blog and found a post where he basically threatened to cut a certain Female X down to size for believing her international fame made her better than her roots."

"Who do you think he was talking about?"

"Well, how many women from Deer Hollow currently have international fame?"

I frowned as I considered his question. "There was Heather Masterson, but she's currently in jail." Heather was a famous local artist who'd recently veered from a life of artistic fame into a life of unexceptional crime.

Hal nodded, eyeing me as if he already knew the answer and was waiting for me to guess. Then it hit me and I almost forgot to breathe. "No!"

His expression turned soothing. "Sheppard is watching their house. He'll follow Lis everywhere until we make sure she's safe."

Tears burned my gaze. It was one more nail in Nancy Villa's coffin. "I just can't believe it, Hal. I grew up with Nancy. She was like a second mother to me. How could she kill a man and go on as if nothing in her life had changed?"

He squeezed my hand. "People will do terrible things in the name of protecting their loved ones."

I looked up at the farmhouse, feeling my chest tighten with dread. "I guess we should go get this over with."

"I can talk to her alone if you'd rather."

I did consider it. Briefly. But then I shook my head. "I need to hear it for myself or I'm afraid I'll never believe it."

We stepped out of the car and started toward the house. I stopped Hal with a hand on his arm before we climbed the wood porch steps, which were painted an ugly blue-gray color. "Betty isn't going to want to say anything that will implicate her cousin."

Hal nodded. "I know. Trust me on this. Okay?"

I realized when I looked up into his dark green

gaze that he was actually asking me if I trusted him. I didn't even hesitate. "I do trust you. More than anything or anyone else."

His answer was a soft smile and a gentle kiss on the lips. "Let's get this over with."

Betty opened the door as we approached. She must have seen us arrive. Her expression was tight, guarded. "Hello, Joey. What a surprise."

I forced a smile. "Hey, Betty. We were hoping you could answer a couple of questions for us."

She stepped out of the house, pressing the ancient wood screen door closed behind her. "If you can walk along with me. I have chores."

I noticed belatedly that she was dressed for farm work. Her small frame was all but overwhelmed by a pair of denim overalls she wore over a plain cotton t-shirt. The cuffs were rolled up to the middle of her slender calves and dirty sneakers covered her small feet. She tugged a wide-brimmed straw hat off a hook on the wall and dropped it onto her head. "Let's go."

We walked around the house and headed toward the barn. Betty walked so quickly I had to nearly run to keep up. Hal's long strides kept up fairly easily, but even he had to make an effort not to fall behind.

I would have wondered what Betty was running from but I already had a pretty good idea. She was running from the questions she knew we were going to ask.

Or, I should say, the questions Hal was going to ask. I was much too breathless from the fast pace to ask any questions.

"This is a great property," Hal said.

She turned a smile on him. "Thanks. My family's been on this land for several generations. It's been a bit of a struggle lately to keep it all going. But I manage."

"Do you farm the place on your own?"

She nodded. "I do."

"What crops do you grow?" Hal asked, his manner easy and his tone sincere. I got the impression he really was interested in the answers to his questions. I could only hope Betty got that same idea.

"Corn and soybeans mostly. I have a garden behind the house where I grow vegetables and some berries which I sell at the farmer's market."

"And the eggs, of course," Hal said with a smile.

"Yes. Actually, that's working out much better than I'd hoped. People like the idea of buying local organic eggs from folks they know and trust."

"I can imagine," he said.

As we got closer to the barn, I was pleased to see just how big it was. I smiled, realizing that at least *that* recollection from my childhood had been accurate.

"How long have you and your cousin been selling the eggs?" Hal asked.

Betty stopped mid-stride and glared up at him. "Nancy didn't kill Viper Branch."

Hal's handsome face showed no emotion. He held her gaze with a neutral one of his own. Finally, he said. "Then your information will only help us clear her name."

For a long moment, Betty's mouth worked over words she couldn't seem to speak. Then she sighed, crossing her arms over her chest. "Branch knew something about Lis. Something that wasn't really that big of a deal, but which would harm her reputation if the modeling world got wind of it."

"What kind of thing?" Hal asked.

Betty shook her head. "It's not important."

"Please, Betty," I said, surprised I could speak through the lump in my throat. "We need to get everything out in the open so we can put an end to this."

I didn't know if that was true. What we discovered was just as likely to extend Nancy and Lis's problems. But I needed to know if Lis was in danger.

Betty frowned at me. "It's actually your fault."

I certainly hadn't been expecting that. "My fault? Why?"

"You encouraged her to pose for that crazy artist and breach her contract with TopNotch Model Management."

"Wait, posing for that painting breached her contract?" I asked in shock. "How is that possible?"

"Lis was only eighteen when she signed that contract. Unfortunately, she didn't let anyone else look at it before she signed it. She basically gave them complete control over every promotional avenue she pursues. The agency is well-known for taking advantage of young model hopefuls. And they rule their models with an iron fist. If they found out about that painting and the fact that it ran in the Deer Hollow and Indianapolis papers, they'd sue Lis for millions. They'd destroy her."

My knees felt weak. I couldn't believe that Lis had put herself into that position. And I really couldn't believe that by helping me, my best friend might have destroyed her own career. "I didn't know."

Betty's glare softened. She sighed. "I'm sure Lis didn't either. But she started getting veiled threats from an anonymous source. They were sent to her home and, thinking they might be something Lis needed to know about, Nancy opened them. She's been a wreck about it. When I saw Viper's blog post, I realized he had to be talking about Lis and Nancy and I put two and two together."

Wringing her hands, Betty suddenly jerked into motion and we were forced to move with her. "Nancy wouldn't have killed him. She couldn't have. Mary Willager was literally found with the bloody weapon in her hands. Why are you trying to pin this on Nancy now?"

We rounded the end of the barn and found ourselves looking at a good-sized greenhouse building. It was filled with flowering plants and bushes, and at the center of the space were several wooden towers. They looked to be built from several boxes each, piled on top of one another, and were painted a variety of bright colors.

Without looking back, Betty entered the greenhouse and headed for the towers.

Hal and I stepped in behind her. With half of the building roofed in metal and the other half in plexiglass to allow the sun inside, the building was cooler than I'd expected. Old-growth trees on the roofed side probably helped keep it cooler too. One side of the space was in the sun, but large fans spun lazily from the ceiling to keep the space from getting too warm.

A soft buzzing sound told me the flowers were being tended by bees and the colorful dance of wings on the air drew my attention to a wide variety of butterflies.

It was beautiful. "This is so pretty."

Betty pulled a panel from the top of one of the towers and examined it, nodding and dropping it back into the box. "I keep the bees in this building so I can control what kind of honey they make. I've handpicked each of the flowers inside this greenhouse."

She slid a glance filled with pride around the

space, seemingly oblivious to the bees swarming unthreateningly around her.

"Aren't you worried about being stung?" I asked.

She shook her head, moving down the aisle to pluck at a few weeds inside the raised beds. "Honey bees don't sting unless they feel threatened."

We watched her fuss over her flowers for a moment, and then Hal brought us back to the subject which had brought us there. "Betty, do you believe your cousin would have killed Viper Branch to protect her daughter?"

Betty stilled, straightening, and sighed. "You aren't going to let this go, are you?"

"Our job is to find a killer," Hal said gently. "I understand how difficult this is for you."

She jerked her head once in the affirmative. Then she gave them a sad smile. "Will you excuse me for just a minute?"

She turned and walked briskly toward the door we'd entered.

Hal and I shared a look.

I glanced at Betty as she stopped just inside the door and reached into a bed there, tugging something from the dirt. "Betty, I know how you feel..."

The other woman straightened up, jerking a shotgun up with her and pointing it at Hal and me. "I'm really sorry, Joey," she said, her eyes glistening with tears. "You should have just heeded my warning and let this all go."

I lifted my hands in a silent plea as she cocked the shotgun, but Hal threw himself at me and we hit the ground as the gun exploded. My hip hit the corner of a raised flower bed and agony speared through me, making it hard to breathe.

The sound of splintering wood preceded the slamming of the door and I just had time to breathe a sigh of relief that she'd missed her mark before the thunderous sound of hundreds of airborne bees inserted itself into my awareness.

That was when I realized she hadn't missed at all.

16

They descended on us in a roiling, stinging swarm, catching in my hair, buzzing inside my ears, and trying to climb up my nose. I screamed but then slammed my mouth closed as bees tried to get past my lips.

Curling into a fetal position, I lay there screaming internally as stinging pain found my exposed skin from my feet all the way to the top of my skull. Something behind me shifted and the bees reared up in agitation, and then a heavy weight descended on me. The sun slipped away and the buzzing was dimmed as Hal's familiar heat washed over me.

I risked opening my eyes and saw that Hal had covered us with some kind of tarp.

A few, trapped bees still flailed against my legs, but I slapped at them, ending their enraged assault.

"Are you okay?" Hal asked, his hand shoving hair off my face.

I nodded. "I feel like a human pincushion. But I'm still alive. That's something, right?"

"You're not allergic to bees?"

"No." I had a sudden thought, trying to turn to get a look at him. "Are you?"

The barest hesitation before he responded told me all I needed to know. "We need to get out of here."

"It's okay. I'm not deathly allergic. Just a little."

"With this many bites, there's no such thing as a little allergic to bees," I told him, already starting to move. "Let's crawl so we can keep this tarp over us for as long as possible."

Movement against my shoulder told me he'd nodded. We started off, an awkward procession that had us heading the wrong direction until we peeked out from the tarp and saw our mistake.

Once we'd adjusted, it took us another several minutes to work our way to the door.

By that point, Hal was wheezing and I was really getting worried we wouldn't get him to the hospital in time.

Then I remembered my phone. I tugged it out of my pocket and dialed.

"9-1-1. What is the address of your emergency?"

"The Weldt Farm, off Highway 37. I need an ambulance to this location right away. My friend was attacked by bees and he's having trouble breathing."

"I'm dispatching an ambulance to that location right now. Please stay on the line until they get there. What is your name, ma'am?"

"I can't stay on the line. I need to call the police."

"I can dispatch the Sheriff's department for you, but I need you to stay on the line until help arrives."

"Just hurry, please?" I shoved the phone into my pocket, not caring if it disconnected or not.

Hal reached up and turned the door handle but the door wouldn't open. He tried to stand up, but his chest was heaving and his lips were a startling blue color.

In desperation, I finally threw off the tarp and flung myself at the door, hearing a small sound as the framing cracked. I threw myself at the door several more times but it was no use. I didn't have enough body weight.

Bees swarmed in our direction, a writhing, buzzing cacophony of rage that I could do nothing to stop.

I kicked the door near the handle as hard as I could.

Nothing.

I wasn't heavy enough to break through. I should have eaten more dang pie!

The tarp rustled and Hal was suddenly there. "Step...aside..." he wheezed.

I did as he asked, knowing if we didn't get out of there, Hal wasn't going to survive. To make things worse, my throat felt tight and I was starting to wheeze too.

It took him three tries to blast the door open. He fell out onto the dusty dirt and I wasn't sure I was going to get him back up again.

"Hal, come on, we need to get to the car."

He forced himself to his feet, his face a swollen mask with angry red welts covering it. I barely recognized him.

I was pretty sure I looked the same.

We started walking, with Hal leaning pretty heavily on me. As I looked toward the distant farmhouse, my heart sank. He'd never make it all the way there.

I was going to lose him!

I looked around for a vehicle of some kind and saw nothing. Then I eyed the barn. "Hal, sit here and rest. I'm going to see if there's some kind of vehicle in the barn."

The fact that he didn't argue told me all I needed to know. Hal was in bad shape.

My wheezing grew as I ran toward the barn doors. My skin was on fire and I felt like somebody had inserted an air pump into my ear and inflated me like a balloon.

Still, I was in much better shape than Hal and he

needed me. So I ran on, fighting to pull air into my lungs.

The doors were open a crack, but it took every ounce of energy I had to pull them wide. By the time I opened them enough to slide through, I was covered in oily sweat and my lungs hurt from struggling to breathe.

But my efforts were rewarded. An old, dusty work vehicle sat in front of the door, and the key was in the ignition.

Now all I had to do was get Hal into the thing.

M oments later, as we roared up on the Weldt family home, we were more dead than alive. Hope soared when I saw Arno standing there with Betty, his hands flying as he seemed to be arguing with her. When they spotted us coming, Betty turned and started to run, but another deputy, Sheppard I thought but I couldn't see him very well, ran her down and tackled her to the ground.

The ambulance roared into the yard, lights and sirens blaring, as I slammed my foot onto the brake and all but fell out of the utility vehicle.

Arno ran over and caught me before my butt hit the dirt.

"Joey?" The question in his voice answered my earlier question. He didn't even recognize me under all the swelling. "Help Hal…" I gasped out.

EMTs ran over to us with epi-pens clutched in their hands. One of them huddled over Hal while one shoved Arno aside and slammed his pen against my thigh.

Within minutes my breathing had improved and, despite some coughing, I was starting to feel human again.

The EMTs had wasted no time getting me onto a stretcher and they were wheeling me toward the ambulance before I was able to ask. "Hal?"

The young woman near my head patted my shoulder. "Your friend will be fine. But right now we need to get you both to the hospital."

I lay back, sighing in relief. I could live with some hospital time, as long as I knew Hal was going to be all right.

I sat in the chair next to Hal's bed, my hospital gown bunching up around my knees as I struggled to keep the slit in the back closed. "I hate these things," I mumbled to Hal.

He licked his lips, his eyes lidded from the anti-histamines they'd been giving him. "I'm glad you're feeling well enough to get mad at your gown," he murmured in a gritty voice.

I heard footsteps behind me and turned to find Arno framed in the doorway, his fist lifted to knock. "Come on in, Arno."

He strode over, looking down at Hal and lifting one blond brow in judgement. "You still look terrible."

Hal chuckled. "So do you, but at least I can blame a hundred bee stings for my looks."

Arno cracked a grin. "Point taken." He scrubbed a big hand over his face. "Well, it's done. Betty Weldt admitted she killed Viper Branch and tried to frame my mom for it."

"That's horrible," I said, shaking my head. "How could she do that?"

"She'd convinced herself Mom would just go to a memory care unit somewhere rather than jail. She was banking on her being my mother and the whole 'not remembering killing him' thing to keep her from incarceration."

"Cold," Hal said in his broken voice.

Arno nodded. "Apparently, Nancy had mentioned a couple of times that she'd run into Mom in the yard at night, confused and not remembering how she'd gotten there. Betty decided to use that to her advantage. She took the knife from Mom's place earlier that day..."

"Wait! What about Nancy saying she wasn't in the neighborhood when GPS said she was?" I asked him.

"She wasn't there, but her car was."

"Betty," Hal croaked out.

Arno nodded. "She borrowed Nancy's car all the time, apparently. All she had was that trike so if she had to buy supplies or if the weather was bad…"

"Nancy would let her drive her car. And since Nancy was sick that day it would have been easy for Betty to take the car without her knowing."

"Yes. Then there was the honey."

I nodded, remembering the rhododendron bushes inside the greenhouse. "She made her own Mad Honey just to poison Spunky."

"Half right. She did make it and fed it to the dog. But she was selling it too. There's apparently a market for honey that gives you hallucinations." He shook his head. "She also added some to Mom's tea that evening. Nancy had mentioned having tea with Mom after the flower committee meetings so Betty knew it was a regular thing. All it took was for her to drop by with honey and offer to add some to Mom's tea. She added enough to give mom a hallucinogenic reaction but not enough to make her sick."

"Diabolical," I said.

"But why'd she kill Branch?" Hal asked.

"Because he broke her personal code. You don't go

after people's family. Betty had grown up with an abusive father, just like Branch. But she survived those years because of her mother's positive outlook and constant refrain of; respect family, love family, protect family. It was her mother's way of coping, I guess. But she created a powerful suggestion in her daughter's brain that ended up being Viper Branch's downfall."

"If only she'd respected *your* family," I said angrily.

"Ironic, huh?" He shook his head. "She admitted to the fire too. She would have burned the garage down along with the house, but she realized, too late, that I was at my mom's. I'd pulled the truck into Mom's garage so I could load stuff into it. She didn't realize I was there until she saw me run out. She took off running toward the woods behind Branch's place. I guess she'd parked the next street over and had walked through the woods. That's why nobody saw her."

"And the warning at Joey's house?" Hal asked, though Betty had all but admitted that.

"Chicken blood," Hal said, grimacing. She was just trying to warn you off because she sensed you were getting too close." He grinned. "I guess she underestimated you, Joey."

I beamed proudly at him. "I guess she did."

We all thought about that for a moment and then Arno shook himself out of his thoughts. "Anyway. Thanks for clearing my mom. I couldn't have done it without you."

"Yeah, you could have," Hal told him. "But fortunately, you didn't have to."

Arno nodded, his expression showing how touched he was by the support. "I'll get out of here and let you rest."

"How are Caphy, LaLee, and Spunky?" I asked Arno. He'd taken the pets to his home when Hal and I had been admitted to the hospital.

"Fine," he said, grinning. "Great, in fact. I'm really enjoying them."

"Even LaLee?" I asked, astonished.

He chuckled. "She's not so bad when you get used to her."

That was high praise coming from Arno.

"I'll come over and get them later today. Lis is picking me up as soon as I'm released." Unfortunately, Hal was going to have to stay another night.

Arno nodded. "I'll be home. I'm moving Mom into my house today."

My eyes went wide. "Really? That's…" I hesitated, not knowing what that was. Daunting? Sad? Terrifying?

He seemed to understand my struggle. "I know it's going to be hard. But now that I know what she's been going through, I want to be there in case she needs my help." He waved goodbye and I couldn't help thinking that Betty wasn't the only one who was willing to go to extraordinary measures to protect family.

My respect for my friend rose even higher than it had been before.

And that was saying something.

THE END

READ MORE COUNTRY COUSINS

Did you enjoy **Spunky Bumpkin**? As my gift to you, enjoy Chapter One of **Rudolph the Red-Nosed Bumpkin**, Book 4: Country Cousin Mysteries.

Rudolph the Red-Nosed Bumpkin, died a very shiny death...

    Rudy-Bob Hortmann has never quite gotten the hang of making friends. He doesn't much like peopling, mostly preferring the company of his pot-bellied pig, Ethel Squeaks to humanoid types. But there's one exception. Rudy-Bob loves kids. So for Christmas every year he gives himself a present. He plays Santa at the annual Deer Hollow Christmas party. Only this year, Rudy-Bob doesn't make it out of the Santa suit when the Pageant is done. Instead,

Deputy Sheriff Arno Willager finds Rudy-Bob literally chillin' in a snowbank, his bulbous nose flashing red through the snow.

That's where I come into the picture. I'm Joey Fulle, and I'm pretty good at finding bodies around my place on the outskirts of Deer Hollow. I didn't actually find this one, of course. But I'm fully invested in locating his killer. 'Cause, with the help of my handsome PI boyfriend Hal, my sweet and goofy Pitbull Caphy, and my opinionated Siamese cat, LaLee, I'm also pretty good at finding killers. Sometimes, even before they find me...

Get **Rudolph the Red-Nosed Bumpkin** at https://samcheever.com/books/#Country

RUDOLPH THE RED-NOSED BUMPKIN

CHAPTER ONE

Imagine my surprise when I walked into my house after the Christmas party at Deer Hollow Town Hall and found my blonde, green-eyed Pitbull, Caphy frothing at the mouth with bright green frosting, and my sophisticated and elegant Siamese cat, LaLee draped glassy-eyed over a branch of the Christmas tree, a pink yarn ball cuddled in her arms like a precious bundle of joy.

I looked from one to the other, unsure what to address first. Behind me, I could feel shock radiating off Hal and knew without looking that he was gawking at the cat.

Never in my wildest dreams would I have ever suspected LaLee had it in her to be goofy. But then I'd never gotten her a catnip ball before.

I grimaced at the sight of her long limbs hanging limply over the branch and scanned a horrified look at the broken ornaments on the floor beneath her. "Oh no!" I hurried over, picking up the adorable Pitbull ornament my friend Lis had bought me the first Christmas Caphy and I had shared together.

I frowned at the cat, whose lids drooped as if she'd been drinking whiskey-spiked eggnog all day. "Bad, kitty!"

LaLee purred even louder, trying to roll over on the wimpy branch and wrapping her long legs even tighter around the ball.

Hal took the broken ornament from me. His handsome face folded into a frown as he examined it, his dark green gaze sliding to mine. "I think I can glue it back together."

I nodded. "Look at this fool cat. She's huggin' that catnip ornament like a drunk hugs a bottle of hooch."

Hal gave me a one-armed hug. "Maybe we should put it into a paper bag for her."

"Har," I said, grinning. "Stupid cat." I reached to pluck her out of the tree, but as soon as I tried to lift her free, her gaze sharpened and she yowled, swiping me with a claw and drawing blood down my arm in a long scratch.

I jerked my arm back. "Ouch!"

LaLee's sudden movement over-balanced her and she slipped off the branch. She scrabbled for purchase, her claws shredding a couple of my silk-covered bulbs and dragging the string of old-fashioned boiling candlesticks down with her.

Her catnip ball stuck in the tree as she fell.

LaLee hit the wrapped presents beneath the tree and immediately sprang up with another yowl, trying to leap back up to reclaim her catnip ball.

Unfortunately for her, I was faster.

I ripped the ornament off the branch and held it above my head as she leaped, slashing at the air beneath the prize.

It was only a matter of time before those claws connected with flesh. I panicked, looking at Hal. "Here!" I threw it at him and his dark green gaze went wide as he caught it, bobbled it a few times in his panic, and then made a small sound of alarm as the cat turned her attention to him.

"Oh no," he murmured, starting to backtrack as the catnip-crazed cat stalked in his direction, a growl vibrating her narrow chest.

"Run!" I told Hal and giggled as he took off like a shot, LaLee five feet behind him and gaining fast.

Hal leaped off the floor and hit the couch, his stocking feet hitting the cushion and leaping the back, only to find himself looking into the cat's feral gaze when he landed.

She'd leaped from the floor onto the back of the couch, foregoing the first step that would have slowed her down.

Caphy stood in the entryway, tail enthusiastically wagging as she watched the show. Hal jerked his arm away with a shout, barely avoiding a swipe of the razor-sharp claws, and Caphy barked gleefully, her nails making a happy clicking sound on the tile.

"Get the door," Hal yelled, jumping sideways and leaping the coffee table to dodge around the outside of the room and run for the front door.

With a shriek, I took off running, Hal with his dangerous baggage held high barreling in my direction.

I managed to wrench the door open just as he skidded across the tiles, and Hal threw the offending yarn ball through the open door, into the night.

LaLee might have been under the influence, but she wasn't stupid. She hated snow and cold with the heat of a thousand suns. She threw on the brakes three feet from the door and skidded all the way to the threshold, a disappointed yowl wafting out into the snowy night and dying under the weight of the Winter storm.

With a delighted bark, Caphy shot past her, nearly blowing her off her drugged feet, and bounced out into the snow to retrieve the ball.

I quickly shut the door behind her. I figured it would take her all of about thirty seconds to shred the stupid ball out there.

I'd retrieve the bits and pieces in the Spring.

Hal held his hand up and I slapped my palm against it.

"Note to self, my cat is a catnip addict. Never buy her catnip toys."

There was a scratch on the front door. I opened it and Caphy trotted in looking proud and happy, pink yarn hanging from her face to mingle with the frosting. She stopped inside the door and shook herself, throwing snow all over Hal and me and my poor tile.

I sighed. "I guess we might as well go see the damage in the kitchen."

"I'll get some paper towels for this floor," Hal said.

I nodded, tucking a long strand of red-blonde hair behind my ear. "I'm afraid to see how many cookies she ate." I'd been a baking maniac for days, baking cookies to gift all my friends and a few dozen for the town Christmas party we'd attended that night. As usual, the party had really put me into the holiday spirit, filled with food, friends, sugar and all my favorite Christmas songs.

I'd enjoyed watching all the kids climb up on Santa's lap, not one of them suspecting who really lived beneath the hat and beard. If they had, they would have asked where Ethel Squeaks, his beloved pot-bellied pig was.

Rudy Hortmann would have no doubt loved to bring his pig to the party, but having her there would have given him away. Everybody in Deer Hollow knew how much Rudy loved that pig. Even the kids would have seen beyond the beard and red velvet suit if he'd had Ethel Squeaks sitting next to him on the dais.

We entered the kitchen to find colorful cardboard strewn across the floor, the remains of the tissue paper I'd cushioned the baked goodies with providing colorful confetti among the ripped and shredded cookie box corpse.

What we didn't find was a single cookie crumb. My naughty pibl hadn't allowed a single grain of sugar to escape her ravenous appetite.

"Well, it looks like she only got hold of Lis's box," Hal said, quickly taking stock of the carefully compiled boxes on the counter.

Caphy wilted under my steely blue glare, her guilt a finely-honed thing that she'd had years of misbehavior to perfect. Unfortunately for me and my cookies, guilt wasn't enough to keep her from misbehaving in the first place.

Lucky for my sweet pibl, she was much too cute for me to stay mad. And, glancing toward my bleeding arm, at least she was smart enough to look guilty. Unlike the snotty feline I could see bathing on the windowsill as if she'd never done violence against me and embarrassed herself hanging in the tree like a drunk.

"You need to put something on that scratch," Hal told me, taking my arm and examining it carefully.

"It's not very deep. I'm fine."

He shook his dark head, kissing me on the nose. "Cat's claws are full of germs. If you don't clean and put something on that, it's going to get infected."

Sighing, I took a look at the mess on the floor.

"This will wait a couple of minutes," Hal assured me. "Caphy and I will get started on it while you're gone."

He wasn't joking about that. My adorable pibl was happily ripping a piece of white tissue paper into pieces and eating it.

I sighed. "Don't let her eat too much of that paper. She's going to be horking it up all night."

He nodded, grinning. "If she's up horking all night it will more than likely be from the dozen Christmas cookies she ate than from that paper."

"Or the catnip and string," I mused, shaking my head. "It's a wonder she's survived as long as she has. That dog will eat anything."

I heard Hal's phone ring as I headed upstairs. I quickly dressed the wound and took a moment to change into comfy clothes and brush my hair before heading back down to the kitchen.

LaLee met me on the bottom stair and rubbed against my ankles, purring as if she hadn't tried to eat me in favor of her drug of choice.

"Yeah, nice try, girlfriend. I'm gonna need a minute to forgive you for slicing my arm open and your general killer attitude."

Hal had a half-full trash bag in one hand and his cell phone in the other. He looked up as I came into the room. "Yeah, I'm at Joey's. Should we meet you there?"

He listened for a beat and then nodded. "We'll be there in five minutes."

"What's up?" I asked, not thrilled at the idea of going back out into the winter wonderland. I'd been looking forward to making some hot chocolate with tiny marshmallows and cuddling on the couch to watch the snow come down beyond the windows.

Hal frowned. "I'm afraid it's bad news. Arno found a body in the snow not too far from here."

Grab your copy of Rudolph the Red-Nosed Bumpkin here: https://samcheever.com/books/rudolph-the-red-nosed-bumpkin/

ALSO BY SAM CHEEVER

If you enjoyed **Spunky Bumpkin**, you might also enjoy these other fun mystery series by Sam. To find out more, visit the **BOOKS** page at www.samcheever.com:

Gainfully Employed Mysteries
Country Cousin Mysteries (**For more Joey, Hal, and Caphy mysteries**)
Honeybun Heat Series
Silver Hills Cozy Mysteries
Yesterday's Paranormal Mysteries
Reluctant Familiar Paranormal Mysteries
Enchanting Inquiries Paranormal Mysteries

DON'T MISS OUT

Stay up on all Sam's news by joining her newsletter,
and get a copy of a fun mystery just for signing up!

SIGN UP HERE!

ABOUT THE AUTHOR

USA Today and Wall Street Journal Bestselling Author Sam Cheever writes mystery and suspense, creating stories that draw you in and keep you eagerly turning pages. Known for writing great characters, snappy dialogue, and unique and exhilarating stories, Sam is the award-winning author of 80+ books.

To learn more about Sam and her work, visit her at one of her online hotspots:
www.samcheever.com
samcheever@samcheever.com